Clarice Lispector

The Imitation of the Rose

Translated by
Katrina Dodson

Edited by
Benjamin Moser

PENGUIN CLASSICS
an imprint of
PENGUIN BOOKS

PENGUIN CLASSICS

UK | USA | Canada | Ireland | Australia
India | New Zealand | South Africa

Penguin Books is part of the Penguin Random House group of companies
whose addresses can be found at global.penguinrandomhouse.com.

First published in the United States of America by New Directions 2015
First published in Great Britain by Penguin Classics 2015
This selection published in Little Clothbound Classics 2023
001

Cover design and illustration by Coralie Bickford-Smith

Clarice Lispector copyright © Heirs of Clarice Lispector, 1951,
1955, 1960, 1965, 1978, 2010, 2015
Translation copyright © Katrina Dodson, 2015

Set in 9.5/13pt Baskerville 10 Pro
Typeset by Jouve (UK), Milton Keynes
Printed and bound in Great Britain by Clays Ltd, Elcograf S.p.A.

The authorized representative in the EEA is Penguin Random House Ireland,
Morrison Chambers, 32 Nassau Street, Dublin D02 YH68

A CIP catalogue record for this book is available from the British Library

ISBN: 978-0-241-63084-6

The Imitation of the Rose

Contents

The Imitation of the Rose

Before Armando got home from work the house had better be tidy and she already in her brown dress so she could tend to her husband while he got dressed, and then they'd leave calmly, arm in arm like the old days. How long since they had done that?

But now that she was 'well' again, they'd take the bus, she gazing out the window like a wife, her arm in his, and then they'd have dinner with Carlota and João, reclining comfortably in their chairs. How long since she had seen Armando at last recline comfortably and have a conversation with a man? A man's peace lay in forgetting about his wife, discussing the latest headlines with another man. Meanwhile she'd chat with Carlota about women's stuff, giving in to Carlota's authoritative and practical benevolence, receiving again at last her friend's inattention and vague disdain, her natural bluntness, and no more of that perplexed and overly curious affection – and at last seeing Armando forget about his wife. And she herself, at last, returning gratefully to insignificance. Like a cat who stayed out all night and, as if nothing had happened, finds a saucer of milk waiting without a word. People were luckily helping her feel she was now 'well.' Without looking at her, they were actively helping her forget, pretending they themselves had forgotten as if they'd read the same label on the same medicine bottle. Or they really had forgotten, who knows. How long since she had seen Armando at last recline with abandon, forget about her? And as for her?

Breaking off from tidying the vanity, Laura looked at herself in the mirror: and as for her, how long had it been? Her face held a domestic charm, her hair was pinned back behind her large, pale ears. Her brown eyes, brown hair, her tawny, smooth skin, all this lent her no longer youthful face a modest, womanly air. Would anyone happen to see, in that tiniest point of surprise lodged in the depths of her eyes, would anyone see in that tiniest offended speck the lack of the children she'd never had?

With her meticulous penchant for method – the same that compelled her as a student to copy the lesson's main points in perfect handwriting without understanding them – with her penchant for method, now taken back up, she was planning to tidy the house before the maid's day off so that, once Maria was gone, she wouldn't have to do anything else, except 1) calmly get dressed; 2) wait for Armando ready to go; 3) what was three? Right. That's exactly what she'd do. And she'd put on the brown dress with the cream lace collar. Already showered. Back at Sacré Coeur she'd been tidy and clean, with a penchant for personal hygiene and a certain horror of messiness.

Which never made Carlota, already back then a bit original, admire her. Their reactions had always been different. Carlota ambitious and laughing heartily: she, Laura, a little slow, and as it were careful always to stay slow; Carlota not seeing the danger in anything. And she ever cautious. When they'd been assigned to read the *Imitation of Christ*, she'd read it with a fool's ardor without understanding but, God forgive her, she'd felt that whoever imitated Christ would be lost – lost in the light, but dangerously lost. Christ was the worst temptation. And Carlota hadn't even wanted to read it, she lied to the nun saying she had. Right. She'd put on the brown dress with the real lace collar.

But when she saw the time she remembered, with a jolt that made her lift her hand to her chest, that she'd forgotten to drink her glass of milk.

She went to the kitchen and, as if in her carelessness she'd guiltily betrayed Armando and her devoted friends, while still at the refrigerator she drank the first sips with an anxious slowing, concentrating on each sip faithfully as if making amends to them all and repenting. Since the doctor had said: 'Drink milk between meals, avoid an empty stomach because it causes anxiety' – so, even without the threat of anxiety, she drank it without a fuss sip by sip, day after day, without fail, obeying with her eyes closed, with a slight ardor for not discerning the slightest skepticism in herself. The awkward thing was that the doctor seemed to contradict himself when, while giving

3

a precise order that she wished to follow with a convert's zeal, he'd also said: 'Let yourself go, take it easy, don't strain yourself to make it work – forget all about what happened and everything will fall back into place naturally.' And he patted her on the back, which flattered her and made her blush with pleasure. But in her humble opinion one order seemed to cancel the other, as if they'd asked her to eat flour and whistle at the same time. To combine them she'd recently resorted to a trick: that glass of milk that had ended up gaining a secret power, every sip of which contained the near-taste of a word and renewed that firm pat on the back, she'd take that glass of milk into the living room, where she'd sit 'very naturally,' pretending not to care at all, 'not straining herself' – and thereby cleverly carrying out the second order. 'It doesn't matter if I gain weight,' she thought, looks had never been the point.

She sat on the sofa like a guest in her own house that, so recently regained, tidy and cool, evoked the tranquility of someone else's house. Which was so satisfying: unlike Carlota, who had made of her home something akin to herself, Laura took such pleasure in making her house an impersonal thing; somehow perfect for being impersonal.

Oh how good it was to be back, really back, she smiled in satisfaction. Holding the nearly empty glass, she closed her eyes with a sigh of pleasant fatigue. She'd ironed Armando's shirts, drawn up methodical lists for the next day, minutely calculated how much she'd spent at the market that morning, hadn't stopped in fact for even a second. Oh how good it was to be tired again.

If a perfect person from the planet Mars landed and discovered that Earthlings got tired and grew old, that person would feel pity and astonishment. Without ever understanding what was good about being human, in feeling tired, in giving out daily; only the initiated would comprehend this subtlety of defectiveness and this refinement of life.

And she'd finally returned from the perfection of the planet Mars. She, who had never cherished any ambition besides being a man's wife, was gratefully reencountering the part of her that gave out daily. With her eyes shut she sighed in appreciation. How long since she had got tired? But now every day she felt nearly exhausted and had ironed, for example, Armando's shirts, she'd always enjoyed ironing and, modesty aside, had a knack for it. And then she'd be exhausted as a reward. No longer that alert lack of fatigue. No longer that empty and wakeful and horribly marvelous speck inside her. No longer that terrible independence. No longer the monstrous and simple ease of not sleeping – day or night – which in its discreet way had made her suddenly superhuman compared to a tired and perplexed husband. He, with that bad breath he got whenever he went mute with worry, which gave her a pungent compassion, yes, even within her wakeful perfection, compassion and love, she superhuman and tranquil in her gleaming isolation, and he, whenever he'd come to visit timidly bearing apples and grapes that the nurse would eat with a shrug, he paying formal visits like a boyfriend, with his unfortunate bad breath and stiff smile, straining heroically to comprehend, he who had received her from a father and a priest, and had no idea what to do with this girl from Tijuca who had unexpectedly, as a tranquil boat bursts into sail on the waters, become superhuman.

Now, no more of this. Never again. Oh, it had just been a bout of weakness; genius was the worst temptation. But afterward she'd returned so completely that she'd even had to start being careful again not to wear people down with her old penchant for detail. She clearly remembered her classmates at Sacré Coeur saying to her: 'You've told it a thousand times!' she recalled with an embarrassed smile. She'd returned so completely: now she got tired every day, every day her face would sag at dusk, and then night would take on its former purpose, it wasn't just the perfect starlit night. And everything lined up harmoniously. And, as with everyone else, each day wore her out; like everyone else, human and perishable. No longer that perfection, no longer that youth. No longer that thing that one day had spread brightly, like a cancer, to her soul.

She opened her sleep-laden eyes, feeling the nice solid glass in her hands, but closed them again with a comfortable smile of fatigue, bathing like some nouveau riche in all her particles, in that familiar and slightly nauseating water. Yes, slightly nauseating; what did it matter, since she too was a bit nauseating, she was well aware. But her husband didn't think so, and so what did it matter, since thank God she didn't live in an environment that required her to be more clever and interesting, and she'd even freed herself from high school, which had so awkwardly demanded that she stay alert. What did it matter. In fatigue – she'd ironed Armando's shirts, not to mention she'd gone to the farmers' market that morning and lingered there so long, with that pleasure she took in making the most of things – in fatigue there was a nice place for her, the discreet and dulled place from which, so embarrassingly for herself and everyone else, she had once emerged. But, as she kept saying, thank God, she'd returned.

And if she sought with greater faith and love, she would find within her fatigue that even better place called sleep. She sighed with pleasure, in a moment of spiteful mischief tempted to go along with that warm exhalation that was her already somnolent breathing, tempted to doze off for a second. 'Just a second, just one little second!' she begged herself, flattered to be so drowsy, begging pleadingly, as if begging a man, which Armando had always liked.

But she didn't really have time to sleep now, not even for a quick nap – she thought vainly and with false modesty, she was such a busy person! She'd always envied people who said 'I didn't have time' and now she was once again such a busy person: they were going to Carlota's for dinner and everything had to be orderly and ready, it was her first dinner party since coming back and she didn't want to be late, she had to be ready when . . . right, I've already said it a thousand times, she thought sheepishly. Once was enough to say: 'I don't want to be late' – since that reason sufficed: if she had never been able to bear without the utmost mortification being a nuisance to anyone, then now, more than ever, she shouldn't . . . No, there wasn't the slightest doubt: she didn't have time to sleep. What she ought to do, familiarly slipping into that intimate wealth of routine – and it hurt her that Carlota scoffed at her penchant for routine – what she ought to do was 1) wait till the maid was ready; 2) give her money to get meat in the morning, rump roast; how could she explain that the difficulty of finding quality meat really was a good topic of conversation, but if Carlota found out she'd scoff at her; 3) start meticulously showering and getting dressed, fully surrendering to the pleasure of making the most of her time. That brown dress complemented her eyes and its little cream lace collar gave her a childlike quality, like an old-fashioned boy. And, back to the nocturnal peace of Tijuca – no longer that blinding light from those coiffed and perky nurses leaving for their day off after tossing her like a helpless chicken into the abyss of insulin – back to the nocturnal peace of Tijuca, back to her real life: she'd go arm-in-arm with Armando, walking slowly to the bus stop, with those short, thick thighs packed into that girdle making her a 'woman of distinction'; but whenever, upset, she told Armando it was because of an ovarian insufficiency, he, who took pride in his wife's thighs, replied rather cheekily: 'What would I get out of marrying a ballerina?' That was how he replied. You'd never guess, but Armando could sometimes be really naughty, you'd never guess. Once in a while they said the same thing. She explained that it was because of an ovarian insufficiency. So then he'd say: 'What would I get out of marrying a ballerina?' He could be really shameless sometimes, you'd never guess. Carlota would be astonished to learn that they too had a private life and things they never told, but she wouldn't tell, what a shame not to be able to tell, Carlota definitely thought she was just uptight and mundane and a little annoying, and if she had to be careful not to bother other people with details, with Armando she'd sometimes relax and get pretty annoying, which didn't matter because he'd pretend to be listening without really listening to everything she was telling him, which didn't hurt her feelings, she understood perfectly well that her chatter tired people out a bit, but it was nice to be able to explain how she hadn't found any meat even if Armando shook his head and wasn't listening, she and the maid chatted a lot, actually she talked more than the maid, and she was also careful not to pester the maid who sometimes held back her impatience and could get a little rude, it was her own fault because she didn't always command respect.

But, as she was saying, her arm in his, she so short and he tall and slim, but he was healthy thank God, and she a brunette. She was a brunette as she obscurely believed a wife ought to be. To have black or blonde hair was an excess to which she, in her desire to do everything right, had never aspired. Therefore, as for green eyes, it seemed to her that having green eyes would be like keeping certain things from her husband. Not that Carlota exactly gave her reason to gossip, but she, Laura – who if given the chance would defend her fervently, but never got the chance – she, Laura, grudgingly had to agree that her friend had a peculiar and funny way of dealing with her husband, oh not that she acted 'as if they were equals,' as people were doing nowadays, but you know what I mean. And Carlota was even a bit original, she'd even mentioned this once to Armando and Armando had agreed but hadn't thought it mattered much. But, as she was saying, dressed in brown with her little collar . . . – this daydream was filling her with the same pleasure she got from tidying drawers, sometimes she'd even mess them up just to be able to tidy them again.

She opened her eyes, and as if the room had dozed off instead of her, it seemed refreshed and relaxed with its brushed armchairs and the curtains that had shrunk in the last wash, like pants that were too short while the person stood comically peering down at his legs. Oh how nice it was to see everything tidy and dusted again, everything cleaned by her own skillful hands, and so silent, and with a vase full of flowers, like a waiting room. She'd always found waiting rooms lovely, so courteous, so impersonal. How rich normal life was, she who had returned from extravagance at last. Even a vase of flowers. She looked at it.

'Oh they're so lovely,' her heart exclaimed, suddenly a bit childish. They were small wild roses she'd bought at the farmers' market that morning, partly because the man had been so insistent, partly out of daring. She'd arranged them in the vase that very morning, while drinking her sacred ten o'clock glass of milk.

Yet bathed in the light of this room the roses stood in all their complete and tranquil beauty.

I've never seen such pretty roses, she thought with curiosity. And as if she hadn't just had that exact thought, vaguely aware that she'd just had that exact thought and quickly glossing over the awkwardness of realizing she was being a little tedious, she thought in a further stage of surprise: 'Honestly, I've never seen such pretty roses.' She looked at them attentively. But her attention couldn't remain mere attention for long, it soon was transformed into gentle pleasure, and she couldn't manage to keep analyzing the roses, she had to interrupt herself with the same exclamation of submissive curiosity: they're so lovely.

They were some perfect roses, several on the same stem. At some point they'd climbed over one another with nimble eagerness but then, once the game was over, they had tranquilly stopped moving. They were some roses so perfect in their smallness, not entirely in bloom, and their pinkish hue was nearly white. They even look fake! she said in surprise. They might look white if they were completely open but, with their central petals curled into buds, their color was concentrated and, as inside an earlobe, you could feel the redness coursing through them. They're so lovely, thought Laura surprised.

But without knowing why, she was a little embarrassed, a little disturbed. Oh, not too much, it was just that extreme beauty made her uncomfortable.

She heard the maid's footsteps on the kitchen tile and could tell from the hollow sound that she was wearing heels; so she must be ready to leave. Then Laura had a somewhat original idea: why not ask Maria to stop by Carlota's and leave her the roses as a present?

And also because that extreme beauty made her uncomfortable. Uncomfortable? It was a risk. Oh, no, why would it be a risk? They just made her uncomfortable, they were a warning, oh no, why would they be a warning? Maria would give Carlota the roses.

'Dona Laura sent them,' Maria would say.

She smiled thoughtfully: Carlota would think it odd that Laura, who could bring the roses herself, since she wanted to give them as a present, sent them with the maid before dinner. Not to mention she'd find it amusing to get roses, she'd think it 'refined' . . .

'There's no need for things like that between us, Laura!'

her friend would say with that slightly rude bluntness, and Laura would exclaim in a muffled cry of rapture: 'Oh no! no! It's not because you invited us to dinner! it's just that the roses were so lovely I decided on a whim to give them to you!'

Yes, if when the time came she could find a way and got the nerve, that's exactly what she'd say. How was it again that she'd say it? She mustn't forget: she'd say – 'Oh no!' etc. And Carlota would be surprised by the delicacy of Laura's feelings, no one would ever imagine that Laura too had her little ideas. In this imaginary and agreeable scene that made her smile beatifically, she called herself 'Laura,' as if referring to a third person. A third person full of that gentle and crackling and grateful and tranquil faith, Laura, the one with the little real-lace collar, discreetly dressed, Armando's wife, finally an Armando who no longer needed to force himself to pay attention to all of her chattering about the maid and meat, who no longer needed to think about his wife, like a man who is happy, like a man who isn't married to a ballerina.

'I couldn't help but send you the roses,' Laura would say, that third person so, so very . . . And giving the roses was nearly as lovely as the roses themselves.

And indeed she'd be rid of them.

And what indeed would happen then? Ah, yes: as she was saying, Carlota surprised by that Laura who was neither intelligent nor good but who also had her secret feelings. And Armando? Armando would look at her with a healthy dose of astonishment – since you can't forget there's no possible way for him to know that the maid brought the roses this afternoon! – Armando would look fondly on the whims of his little woman, and that night they'd sleep together.

And she'd have forgotten the roses and their beauty.

No, she thought suddenly vaguely forewarned. She must watch out for other people's alarmed stares. She must never again give cause for alarm, especially with everything still so recent. And most important of all was sparing everyone from suffering the least bit of doubt. And never again cause other people to fuss over her – never again that awful thing where everyone stared at her mutely, and her right there in front of everyone. No whims.

But at the same time she saw the empty glass of milk in her hand and also thought: 'he' said not to strain myself to make it work, not to worry about acting a certain way just to prove that I'm already . . .

'Maria,' she then said upon hearing the maid's foot-steps again. And when Maria approached, she said impetuously and defiantly: 'Could you stop by Dona Carlota's and leave these roses for her? Say it like this: "Dona Carlota, Dona Laura sent these." Say it like this: "Dona Carlota . . ."'

'Got it, got it,' said the maid patiently.

Laura went to find an old piece of tissue paper. Then

she carefully took the roses out of the vase, so lovely and tranquil, with their delicate and deadly thorns. She wanted to give the arrangement an artistic touch. And at the same time be rid of them. And she could get dressed and move on with her day. When she gathered the moist little roses into a bouquet, she extended the hand holding them, looked at them from a distance, tilting her head and narrowing her eyes for an impartial and severe judgment.

And when she looked at them, she saw the roses.

And then, stubborn, gentle, she coaxed inwardly: don't give away the roses, they're lovely.

A second later, still very gentle, the thought intensified slightly, almost tantalizing: don't give them away, they're yours. Laura gasped a little: because things were never hers.

But these roses were. Rosy, small, perfect: hers. She looked at them in disbelief: they were beautiful and hers. If she managed to think further, she'd think: hers like nothing else had ever been.

And she could even keep them since she'd already shed that initial discomfort that made her vaguely avoid looking at the roses too much.

Why give them away, then? lovely and you're giving them away? After all when you happen upon a good thing, you just go and give it away? After all if they were hers, she coaxed persuasively without finding any argument besides the one that, with repetition, seemed increasingly convincing and simple. They wouldn't last long – so why give them away while they were still alive? The pleasure of having them didn't pose much of a risk – she deluded herself – after all, whether or not she wanted them, she'd have to give them up soon enough, and then she'd never think of them again since they'd be dead – they wouldn't last long, so why give them away? The fact that they didn't last long seemed to remove her guilt about keeping them, according to the obscure logic of a woman who sins. After all you could see they wouldn't last long (it would be quick, free from danger). And besides – she argued in a final and triumphant rejection of guilt – by no means had she been the one who'd wanted to buy them, the vendor kept insisting and she always got so flustered when people put her on the spot, she hadn't been the one who'd wanted to buy them, she was in no way to blame whatsoever. She looked at them entranced, thoughtful, profound.

And, honestly, I've never seen anything more perfect in all my life.

Fine, but now she'd already spoken to Maria and there was no way to turn back. So was it too late?, she got scared, seeing the little roses waiting impassively in her own hand. If she wanted, it wouldn't be too late . . . She could tell Maria: 'Listen Maria, I've decided to take the roses over myself when I go to dinner!' And, of course, she wouldn't take them . . . And Maria would never have to know. And, before changing clothes, she'd sit on the sofa for a second, just a second, to look at them. And to look at those roses' tranquil detachment. Yes, since, having done the deed, you might as well take advantage of it, wouldn't it be silly to take the blame without reaping the rewards. That's exactly what she'd do.

But with the unwrapped roses in her hand she waited. She wasn't putting them back in the vase, she wasn't calling Maria. She knew why. Because she ought to give them away. Oh she knew why.

And also because a pretty thing was meant for giving or receiving, not just having. And, above all, never just for 'being.' Above all one should never be the pretty thing. A pretty thing lacked the gesture of giving. One should never keep a pretty thing, just like that, as if stowed inside the perfect silence of the heart. (Although, if she didn't give away the roses, no one in the world would ever know that she'd planned to give them away, who would ever find out? it was horribly easy and doable to keep them, since who would ever find out? and they'd be hers, and that would be the end of it and no one would mention it again . . .)

So? and so? she wondered vaguely worried.

So, no. What she ought to do was wrap them up and send them off, without any enjoyment now; wrap them up and, disappointed, send them off; and in astonishment be rid of them. Also because a person must have some consistency, her thinking ought to have some continuity: if she'd spontaneously decided to hand them over to

Carlota, she should stick to her decision and give them away. Because no one changed their mind from one moment to the next.

But anyone can have regrets! she suddenly rebelled. Since it was only the moment I picked the roses up that I realized how beautiful I thought they were, for the very first time in fact, when I picked them up, that's when I realized they were beautiful. Or just before? (And besides they were hers.) And besides the doctor himself had patted her on the back and said: 'Don't strain to pretend you're well, ma'am, because you *are* well,' and then that firm pat on the back. That's why, then, she didn't have to be consistent, she didn't have to prove anything to anyone and she'd keep the roses. (And besides – besides they were hers).

'Are they ready?' asked Maria.

'Yes,' said Laura caught by surprise.

She looked at them, so mute in her hand. Impersonal in their extreme beauty. In their extreme, perfect rose tranquility. That last resort: the flower. That final perfection: luminous tranquility.

Like an addict, she looked with faint greed at the roses' tantalizing perfection, with her mouth slightly dry she looked at them.

Until, slow, austere, she wrapped the stems and thorns in the tissue paper. She had been so absorbed that only when she held out the finished bouquet did she realize that Maria was no longer in the room – and she was left alone with her heroic sacrifice. Vaguely afflicted, she looked at them, remote at the end of her outstretched arm – and her mouth grew still more parched, that envy, that desire. But they're mine, she said with enormous timidity.

When Maria returned and took the bouquet, in a fleeting instant of greed Laura pulled her hand away keeping the roses one second longer – they're lovely and they're mine, it's the first thing that's lovely and mine! plus it was that man who insisted, it wasn't me who went looking for them! fate wanted it this way! oh just this once! just this once and I swear never again! (She could at least take one rose for herself, no more than that: one rose for herself. And only she would know, and then never again oh, she promised herself that never again would she let herself be tempted by perfection, never again!)

And the next second, without any transition at all, without any obstacle at all – the roses were in the maid's hand, they were no longer hers, like a letter already slipped into the mailbox! no more chances to take it back or cross anything out! it was no use crying: that's not what I meant! She was left empty-handed but her obstinate and resentful heart was still saying: 'You can catch Maria on the stairs, you know perfectly well you can, and snatch the roses from her hand and steal them.' Because taking them now would be stealing. Stealing something that was hers? Since that's what someone who felt no pity for others would do: steal something that was rightfully hers! Oh, have mercy, dear God. You can take it all back, she insisted furiously. And then the front door slammed.

Then the front door slammed.

Then slowly she sat calmly on the sofa. Without leaning back. Just to rest. No, she wasn't angry, oh not at all. But that offended speck in the depths of her eyes had grown larger and more pensive. She looked at the vase. 'Where are my roses,' she then said very calmly.

And she missed the roses. They had left a bright space inside her. Remove an object from a clean table and from the even cleaner mark it leaves you can see that dust had been surrounding it. The roses had left a dustless, sleepless space inside her. In her heart, that rose she could at least have taken for herself without hurting anyone in the world was missing. Like some greater lack.

In fact, like the lack. An absence that was entering her like a brightness. And the dust was also disappearing from around the mark the roses left. The center of her fatigue was opening in an expanding circle. As if she hadn't ironed a single one of Armando's shirts. And in the clear space the roses were missed. 'Where are my roses,' she wailed without pain while smoothing the pleats in her skirt.

Like when you squeeze lemon into black tea and the black tea starts brightening all over. Her fatigue was gradually brightening. Without any fatigue whatsoever, incidentally. The way a firefly lights up. Since she was no longer tired, she'd get up and get dressed. It was time to start.

But, her lips dry, she tried for a second to imitate the roses inside herself. It wasn't even hard.

It was all the better that she wasn't tired. That way she'd go to dinner even more refreshed. Why not pin that cameo onto her little real-lace collar that the major had brought back from the war in Italy? It would set off her neckline so nicely. When she was ready she'd hear the sound of Armando's key in the door. She needed to get dressed. But it was still early. He'd be caught in traffic. It was still afternoon. A very pretty afternoon.

Incidentally it was no longer afternoon.

It was night. From the street rose the first sounds of the darkness and the first lights.

Incidentally the key familiarly penetrated the keyhole.

Armando would open the door. He'd switch the light on. And suddenly in the doorframe the expectant face that he constantly tried to mask but couldn't suppress would be bared. Then his bated breath would finally transform into a smile of great unburdening. That embarrassed smile of relief that he'd never suspected she noticed. That relief they had probably, with a pat on the back, advised her poor husband to conceal. But which, for his wife's guilt-ridden heart, had been daily reward for at last having given back to that man the possibility of joy and peace, sanctified by the hand of an austere priest who only allowed beings a humble joy and not the imitation of Christ.

The key turned in the lock, the shadowy and hurried figure entered, light violently flooded the room.

And right in the doorway he froze with that panting and suddenly paralyzed look as if he'd run for miles so as not to get home too late. She was going to smile. So he could at last wipe that anxious suspense off his face, which always came mingled with the childish triumph of getting home in time to find her there boring, nice and diligent, and his wife. She was going to smile so he'd once again know that there would never again be any danger of his getting home too late. She was going to smile to teach him sweetly to believe in her. It was no use advising them never to mention the subject: they didn't talk about it but had worked out a language of facial expressions in which fear and trust were conveyed, and question and answer were mutely telegraphed. She was going to smile. It was taking a while but she was going to smile.

Calm and gentle, she said:

'It's back, Armando. It's back.'

As if he would never understand, his face twisted into a dubious smile. His primary task at the moment was trying to catch his breath after sprinting up the stairs, since he'd triumphantly avoided getting home late, since there she was smiling at him. As if he'd never understand.

'What's back,' he finally asked in a blank tone of voice.

But, as he was trying never to understand, the man's progressively stiffening face had already understood, though not a single feature had altered. His primary task was to stall for time and concentrate on catching his breath. Which suddenly was no longer hard to do. For unexpectedly he realized in horror that both the living room and his wife were calm and unhurried. With even further misgiving, like someone who bursts into laughter after getting the joke, he nonetheless insisted on keeping his face contorted, from which he watched her warily, almost her enemy. And from which he was starting to no longer help noticing how she was sitting with her hands crossed on her lap, with the serenity of a lit-up firefly.

In her brown-eyed and innocent gaze the proud embarrassment of not having been able to resist.

'What's back,' he said suddenly harsh.

'I couldn't help it,' she said, and her final compassion for the man was in her voice, that final plea for forgiveness already mingled with the haughtiness of a solitude almost perfect now. I couldn't help it, she repeated surrendering to him in relief the compassion she had struggled to hold onto until he got home. 'It was because of the roses,' she said modestly.

As if holding still for a snapshot of that instant, he kept that same detached face, as if the photographer had wanted only his face and not his soul. He opened his mouth and for an instant his face involuntarily took on that expression of comic indifference he'd used to hide his mortification when asking his boss for a raise. The next second, he averted his eyes in shame at the indecency of his wife who, blossoming and serene, was sitting there.

But suddenly the tension fell away. His shoulders

23

sagged, his features gave way and a great heaviness relaxed him. He looked at her older now, curious.

She was sitting there in her little housedress. He knew she'd done what she could to avoid becoming luminous and unattainable. Timidly and with respect, he was looking at her. He'd grown older, weary, curious. But he didn't have a single word to say. From the open doorway he saw his wife on the sofa without leaning back, once again alert and tranquil, as if on a train. That had already departed.

Family Ties

The woman and her mother finally squeezed into the taxi that was taking them to the station. The mother kept counting and recounting the two suitcases trying to convince herself that both were in the car. The daughter, with her dark eyes, whose slightly cross-eyed quality gave them a constant glimmer of derision and detachment – watched.

'I haven't forgotten anything?' the mother was asking for the third time.

'No, no, you haven't forgotten anything,' the daughter answered in amusement, patiently.

That somewhat comic scene between her mother and her husband still lingered in her mind, when it came time to say goodbye. For the entire two weeks of the old woman's visit, the two could barely stand each other; their good-mornings and good-afternoons constantly struck a note of cautious tact that made her want to laugh. But right when saying goodbye, before getting into the taxi, her mother had transformed into a model mother-in-law and her husband had become the good son-in-law. 'Forgive any misspoken words,' the old lady had said, and Catarina, taking some joy in it, had seen Antônio fumble with the suitcases in his hands, stammering – flustered at being the good son-in-law. 'If I laugh, they'll think I'm mad,' Catarina had thought, frowning. 'Whoever marries off a son loses a son, whoever marries off a daughter gains a son,' her mother had added, and Antônio took advantage of having the flu to cough. Catarina, standing there, had mischievously observed her husband whose self-assurance gave way to a diminutive, dark-haired man, forced to be a son to that tiny graying woman . . . Just then her urge to laugh intensified. Luckily she never actually had to laugh whenever she got the urge: her eyes took on a sly, restrained look, went even more cross-eyed – and her laughter came out through her eyes. Being able to laugh always hurt a little. But she couldn't help it: ever since she was little she'd laughed through her eyes, she'd always been cross-eyed.

'I'll say it again, that boy is too skinny,' her mother declared while bracing herself against the jolting of the car. And though Antônio wasn't there, she adopted the same combative, accusatory tone she used with him. So much that one night Antônio had lost his temper: 'It's not my fault, Severina!' He called his mother-in-law Severina, since before the wedding he'd envisioned them as a modern mother- and son-in-law. Starting from her mother's first visit to the couple, the word Severina had turned leaden in her husband's mouth, and so, now, the fact that he used her first name hadn't stopped . . . – Catarina would look at them and laugh.

'The boy's always been skinny, Mama,' she replied.
The taxi drove on monotonously.

'Skinny and anxious,' added the old lady decisively.

'Skinny and anxious,' Catarina agreed patiently.

He was an anxious, distracted boy. During his grand-mother's visit he'd become even more remote, slept poorly, was upset by the old woman's excessive affection and loving pinches. Antônio, who'd never been particularly worried about his son's sensitivity, had begun dropping hints to his mother-in-law, 'to protect a child' . . .

'I haven't forgotten anything . . .' her mother started up again, when the car suddenly braked, launching them into each other and sending their suitcases flying. Oh! oh!, shouted her mother as if faced with some irremediable disaster, 'oh!' she said shaking her head in surprise, suddenly older and pitiable. And Catarina?

Catarina looked at her mother, and mother looked at daughter, and had some disaster also befallen Catarina? her eyes blinked in surprise, she quickly righted the suitcases and her purse, trying to remedy the catastrophe as fast as possible. Because something had indeed happened, there was no point hiding it: Catarina had been launched into Severina, into a long forgotten bodily intimacy, going back to the age when one has a father and mother. Though they'd never really hugged or kissed. With her father, yes, Catarina had always been more of a friend. Whenever her mother would fill their plates making them overeat, the two would wink at each other conspiratorially and her mother never even noticed. But after colliding in the taxi and after regaining their composure, they had nothing to talk about – why weren't they already at the station?

'I haven't forgotten anything,' her mother asked in a resigned voice.

Catarina no longer wished to look at her or answer.

'Take your gloves!' she said as she picked them up off the ground.

'Oh! oh! my gloves!' her mother exclaimed, flustered.

They only really looked at each other once the suitcases were deposited on the train, after they'd exchanged kisses: her mother's head appeared at the window.

Catarina then saw that her mother had aged and that her eyes were glistening.

The train wasn't leaving and they waited with nothing to say. The mother pulled a mirror from her purse and studied herself in her new hat, bought at the same milliner's where her daughter went. She gazed at herself while making an excessively severe expression that didn't lack in self-admiration. Her daughter watched in amusement. No one but me can love you, thought the woman laughing through her eyes; and the weight of that responsibility left the taste of blood in her mouth. As if 'mother and daughter' were life and abhorrence. No, you couldn't say she loved her mother. Her mother pained her, that was all. The old woman had slipped the mirror back into her purse, and was smiling steadily at her. Her worn and still quite clever face looked like it was struggling to make a certain impression on the people around her, in which her hat played a role. The station bell suddenly rang, there was a general movement of anxiousness, several people broke into a run thinking the train was already leaving: Mama! the woman said. Catarina! the old woman said. They gaped at each other, the suitcase on a porter's head blocked their view and a young man rushing past grabbed Catarina's arm in passing, jerking the collar of her dress off-kilter. When they could see each other again, Catarina was on the verge of asking if she'd forgotten anything . . .

'. . . I haven't forgotten anything?' her mother asked.

Catarina also had the feeling they'd forgotten something, and they looked at each other at a loss – for if they really had forgotten something, it was too late now. A woman dragged a child along, the child wailed, the station bell resounded again . . . Mama, said the woman. What was it they'd forgotten to say to each other? and now it was too late. It struck her that one day they should have said something like: 'I am your mother, Catarina.' And she should have answered: 'And I am your daughter.'

'Don't sit in the draft!' Catarina called.

'Come now, girl, I'm not a child,' said her mother, never taking her attention off her own appearance. Her freckled hand, slightly tremulous, was delicately arranging the brim of her hat and Catarina suddenly wanted to ask whether she'd been happy with her father:

'Give my best to Auntie!' she shouted.

'Yes, of course!'

'Mama,' said Catarina because a lengthy whistle was heard and the wheels were already turning amid the smoke.

'Catarina!' the old woman called, her mouth open and her eyes astonished, and at the first lurch her daughter saw her raise her hands to her hat: it had fallen over her nose, covering everything but her new dentures. The train was already moving and Catarina waved. Her mother's face disappeared for an instant and immediately reappeared hatless, her loosened bun spilling in white locks over her shoulders like the hair of a maiden – her face was downcast and unsmiling, perhaps no longer even seeing her daughter in the distance.

Amid the smoke Catarina began heading back, frowning, with that mischievous look of the cross-eyed. Without her mother's company, she had regained her firm stride: it was easier alone. A few men looked at her, she was sweet, a little heavyset. She walked serenely, dressed in a modern style, her short hair dyed 'mahogany.' And things had worked out in such a way that painful love seemed like happiness to her – everything around her was so alive and tender, the dirty street, the old trams, orange peels – strength flowed back and forth through her heart in weighty abundance. She was very pretty just then, so elegant; in step with her time and the city where she'd been born as if she had chosen it. In her cross-eyed look anyone could sense the enjoyment this woman took in the things of the world. She stared at other people boldly, trying to fasten onto those mutable figures her pleasure that was still damp with tears for her mother. She veered out of the way of oncoming cars, managed to sidestep the line for the bus, glancing around ironically; nothing could stop this little woman whose hips swayed as she walked from climbing one more mysterious step in her days.

The elevator hummed in the beachfront heat. She opened the door to her apartment while using her other hand to free herself of her little hat; she seemed poised to reap the largess of the whole world, the path opened by the mother who was burning in her chest. Antônio barely looked up from his book. Saturday afternoon had always been 'his,' and, as soon as Severina had left, he gladly reclaimed it, seated at his desk.

'Did "she" leave?'

'Yes she did,' answered Catarina while pushing open the door to her son's room. Ah, yes, there was the boy, she thought in sudden relief. Her son. Skinny and anxious. Ever since he could walk he'd been steady on his feet; but nearing the age of four he still spoke as if he didn't know what verbs were: he'd confirm things coldly, not linking them. There he sat fiddling with his wet towel, exact and remote. The woman felt a pleasant warmth and would have liked to capture the boy forever in that moment; she pulled the towel from his hands

31

disapprovingly: that boy! But the boy gazed indifferently into the air, communicating with himself. He was always distracted. No one had ever really managed to hold his attention. His mother shook out the towel and her body blocked the room from his view: 'Mama,' said the boy. Catarina spun around. It was the first time he'd said 'Mama' in that tone of voice and without asking for anything. It had been more than a confirmation: Mama! The woman kept shaking the towel violently and wondered if there was anyone she could tell what happened, but she couldn't think of anyone who'd understand what she couldn't explain. She smoothed the towel vigorously before hanging it to dry. Maybe she could explain, if she changed the way it happened. She'd explain that her son had said: 'Mama, who is God.' No, maybe: 'Mama, boy wants God.' Maybe. The truth would only fit into symbols, they'd only accept it through symbols. Her eyes smiling at her necessary lie, and above all at her own foolishness, fleeing from Severina, the woman unexpectedly laughed aloud at the boy, not just with her eyes: her whole body burst into laughter, a burst casing, and a harshness emerging as hoarseness. Ugly, the boy then said peering at her.

'Let's go for a walk!' she replied blushing and taking him by the hand.

She passed through the living room, informing her husband without breaking stride: 'We're going out!' and slammed the apartment door.

Antônio hardly had time to look up from his book – and in surprise saw that the living room was already empty. Catarina! he called, but he could already hear the sound of the descending elevator. Where did they go? he wondered nervously, coughing and blowing his nose. Because Saturday was his, but he wanted his wife and his son at home while he enjoyed his Saturday. Catarina! he called irritably though he knew she could no longer hear him. He got up, went to the window and a second later spotted his wife and son on the sidewalk.

The pair had stopped, the woman perhaps deciding which way to go. And suddenly marching off.

Why was she walking so briskly, holding the child's hand? through the window he saw his wife gripping the child's hand tightly and walking swiftly, her eyes staring straight ahead; and, even without seeing it, the man could tell that her jaw was set. The child, with who-knew-what obscure comprehension, was also staring straight ahead, startled and unsuspecting. Seen from above, the two figures lost their familiar perspective, seemingly flattened to the ground and darkened against the light of the sea. The child's hair was fluttering . . .

The husband repeated his question to himself, which, though cloaked in the innocence of an everyday expression, worried him: where are they going? He nervously watched his wife lead the child and feared that just now when both were beyond his reach she would transmit to their son . . . but what exactly? 'Catarina,' he thought,

'Catarina, this child is still innocent!' Just when does a mother, holding a child tight, impart to him this prison of love that would forever fall heavily on the future man. Later on her son, a man now, alone, would stand before this very window, drumming his fingers against this windowpane; trapped. Forced to answer to a dead person. Who could ever know just when a mother passes this legacy to her son. And with what somber pleasure. Mother and son now understanding each other inside the shared mystery. Afterward no one would know from what black roots a man's freedom is nourished. 'Catarina,' he thought enraged, 'that child is innocent!' Yet they'd disappeared somewhere along the beach. The shared mystery.

'But what about me? what about me?' he asked fearfully. They had gone off alone. And he had stayed behind. 'With his Saturday.' And his flu. In that tidy apartment, where 'everything ran smoothly.' What if his wife was fleeing with their son from that living room with its well-adjusted light, from the tasteful furniture, the curtains and the paintings? that was what he'd given her. An engineer's apartment. And he knew that if his wife enjoyed the situation of having a youthful husband with a promising future – she also disparaged it, with those deceitful eyes, fleeing with their anxious, skinny son. The man got worried. Since he couldn't provide her anything but: more success. And since he knew that she'd help him achieve it and would hate whatever they accomplished. That was how this calm, thirty-two-year-old woman was, who never really spoke, as if she'd been alive forever. Their relationship was so peaceful. Sometimes he tried to humiliate her, he'd barge into their bedroom while she was changing because he knew she detested being seen naked. Why did he need to humiliate her? yet he was well aware that she would only ever belong to a man as long as she had her pride. But he had grown used to this way of making her feminine: he'd humiliate her with tenderness, and soon enough she'd smile – without resentment? Maybe this had given rise to the peaceful nature of their relationship, and those muted conversations that created a homey environment for their child. Or would he sometimes get irritable? Sometimes the boy would get irritable, stomping his feet, screaming from nightmares. What had this vibrant little creature been born from, if not from all that he and his wife had cut from their everyday life. They lived so peacefully that, if they brushed up against a moment of joy, they'd exchange rapid, almost ironic, glances, and both would say with their eyes: let's not waste it, let's not use it up frivolously. As if they'd been alive forever.

But he had spotted her from the window, seen her striding swiftly holding hands with their son, and said to himself: she's savoring a moment of joy – alone. He had felt frustrated because for a while now he hadn't been able to live unless with her. And she still managed to savor her moments – alone. For example, what had his wife been up to on the way from the train to the apartment? not that he had any suspicions but he felt uneasy.

The last light of the afternoon was heavy and beat down solemnly on the objects. The dry sands crackled. The whole day had been under this threat of radiating. Which just then, without exploding, nonetheless, grew increasingly deafening and droned on in the building's ceaseless elevator. Whenever Catarina returned they'd have dinner while swatting at the moths. The boy would cry out after first falling asleep, Catarina would interrupt dinner for a moment . . . and wouldn't the elevator let up for even a second?! No, the elevator wouldn't let up for a second.

'After dinner we'll go to the movies,' the man decided. Because after the movies it would be night at last, and this day would shatter with the waves on the crags of Arpoador.

The Crime of the Mathematics Teacher

When the man reached the highest hill, the bells were ringing in the city below. Only the uneven rooftops were in sight. Nearby was the lone tree on the plateau. The man was standing there holding a heavy sack.

He looked down below with nearsighted eyes. The Catholics were entering the church slow and tiny, and he strained to hear the scattered voices of the children dispersed throughout the square. But despite the morning's clearness the sounds barely reached the high plain. He also saw the river that appeared motionless from above, and thought: it's Sunday. In the distance he saw the highest mountain with its dry slopes. It wasn't cold but he drew his sport coat around him more snugly. At last he carefully laid the sack on the ground. He took off his glasses maybe to breathe better since, while holding his glasses, he breathed very deeply. Sunlight hit his lenses, which sent out piercing signals. Without his glasses, his eyes blinked brightly, almost youthful, unfamiliar. He put his glasses back on, became a middle-aged man and picked up the sack again: it was heavy as if made of stone, he thought. He squinted trying to make out the river's current, tilting his head to catch any noises: the river was at a standstill and only the hardier sound of a single voice reached those heights for an instant – yes, he was quite alone. The cool air was inhospitable, since he'd been living in a warmer city. The branches of the lone tree on the plateau swayed. He looked at it. He was biding his time. Until he decided there was no reason to wait any longer.

And nevertheless he waited. His glasses must have been bothering him because he took them off again, breathed deeply and tucked them into his pocket.

He then opened the sack, peered partway into it. Next he put his bony hand inside and started pulling out the dead dog. His whole being was focused solely on that important hand and he kept his eyes deeply shut as he pulled. When he opened them, the air was even brighter and the joyful bells pealed once more summoning the faithful to the solace of punishment.

The unknown dog was out in the open.

Then he set to work methodically. He picked up the stiff, black dog, laid it in a depression in the ground. But, as if he'd already done too much, he put on his glasses, sat beside the dog and started surveying the landscape.

He saw very clearly, and with a certain futility the deserted plateau. But he noted precisely that when seated he could no longer glimpse the town below. He breathed again. He reached back into the sack and pulled out the shovel. And considered which site to choose. Maybe under the tree. He caught himself musing that he'd bury this dog under the tree. But if it were the other one, the real dog, he'd actually bury it where he himself would like to be buried if he were dead: at the very center of the plateau, facing the sun with empty eyes. So, since the unknown dog was standing in for the 'other' one, he wanted it, for the greater perfection of the act, to get exactly what the other would. There was no confusion whatsoever in the man's head. He coldly understood himself, no loose ends.

Soon, being excessively scrupulous, he became highly absorbed in rigorously trying to determine the middle of the plateau. It wasn't easy because the lone tree stood on one side and, marking a false center, divided the plain asymmetrically. Faced with this obstacle the man admitted: 'I didn't need to bury him at the center, I'd have also buried the other one, let's say, right where I'm standing this very second.' Because it was a question of granting the event the fatefulness of chance, the sign of an external and obvious occurrence – similar to the children in the square and the Catholics entering the church – it was a question of rendering the fact as visible as possible on the surface of the world beneath the heavens. It was a question of exposing himself and exposing a fact, and not allowing the intimate and unpunished form of a thought.

At the idea of burying the dog where he was standing that very moment – the man recoiled with an agility that his small and singularly heavy body wouldn't allow. Because it seemed to him that beneath his feet the outline of the dog's grave had been drawn.

So he began digging right there, his shovel rhythmic. Sometimes he'd pause to take his glasses off and put them back on. He was sweating grievously. He didn't dig very deep but not because he wanted to save his energy. He didn't dig very deep because he thought lucidly: 'if it were for the real dog, I'd dig a shallow hole, I'd bury him close to the surface.' He thought that near the surface of the earth the dog wouldn't be deprived of its senses.

Finally he dropped the shovel, gently lifted the unknown dog and placed it in the grave.

What a strange face that dog had. When, with a start he'd come upon the dead dog on a street corner, the idea of burying it had made his heart so heavy and surprised, that he hadn't even noticed that stiff muzzle and crusted drool. It was a strange and objective dog.

The dog came up slightly higher than the hole he had dug and after being covered with dirt it would be a barely discernible mound on the plateau. That was exactly how he wanted it. He covered the dog with dirt and smoothed it over with his hands, feeling its shape under his palms intently and with pleasure as if he were petting it several times. The dog was now merely a feature of the terrain.

Then the man stood, brushed the dirt off his hands, and didn't give the grave another look. He thought with a certain pleasure: I think I've done everything. He gave a deep sigh, and an innocent smile of liberation. Yes, he'd done everything. His crime had been punished and he was free.

And now he could think freely about the real dog. He immediately started thinking about the real dog, which he'd avoided doing up till now. The real dog that even now must be wandering bewilderedly through the streets of the other town, sniffing all over that city where he no longer had a master.

He then started to think with some trouble about the real dog as if he were trying to think with some trouble about his real life. The fact that the dog was far away in that other city troubled the task, though longing brought him closer to its memory.

'While I was making you in my image, you were making me in yours,' he thought then with the aid of longing. 'I gave you the name José to give you a name that would also serve as your soul. And you – how can I ever know what name you gave me? How much more you loved me than I loved you,' he reflected curiously.

'We understood each other too well, you with the human name I gave you, I with the name you gave me that you never spoke except with your insistent gaze,' thought the man smiling tenderly, now free to reminisce as he pleased.

'I remember you when you were little,' he thought amused, 'so small, cute and weak, wagging your tail, looking at me, and I unexpectedly finding in you a new form of having my soul. But, from then on, every day you were already starting to be a dog one could abandon. Meanwhile, our games were getting dangerous from so much understanding,' the man recalled in satisfaction, 'you ended up biting me and growling, I ended up hurling a book at you and laughing. But who knows what that fake laugh of mine meant. Every day you were a dog one could abandon.'

'And how you sniffed at the streets!' thought the man laughing a little, 'you really didn't leave a single stone unsniffed . . . That was your childish side. Or was it your true calling as a dog? and the rest was just playing at being mine? Because you were indomitable. And, calmly wagging your tail, you seemed to reject silently the name I'd given you. Ah, yes, you were indomitable: I didn't want you to eat meat so you wouldn't get ferocious, but one day you leaped onto the table and, as the children happily shouted, snatched the meat and, with a ferocity that doesn't come from what you eat, you stared at me mute and indomitable with the meat in your mouth. Because, though you were mine, you never yielded to me even a little of your past or your nature. And, worried, I started to understand that you didn't demand that I give up anything of mine to love you, and this started to bother me. It was at the endpoint of the stubborn reality of our two natures that you expected us to understand each other. My ferocity and yours shouldn't be exchanged out of sweetness: that was what you taught me little by little, and that too was starting to weigh on me. By not asking anything of me, you asked too much. From yourself, you demanded that you be a dog. From me, you demanded that I be a man. And I, I pretended as best I could. Sometimes, sitting back on your paws in front of me, how you'd stare at me! So I'd look at the ceiling, cough, pretend not to notice, examine my nails. But nothing affected you: you went on staring at me. Who were you going to tell? Pretend – I'd tell myself – quick pretend you're someone else, give a false interview, pet him, throw him a bone – but nothing distracted you: you went on staring at me. What a fool I was. I shuddered in horror, when you were the innocent one: if I turned around and suddenly showed you my true face, and, bristling, hurt, you'd drag yourself over to the door forever wounded. Oh, every day you were a dog one could abandon. One could choose to. But you, trusting, wagged your tail.

'Sometimes, touched by your perceptiveness, I'd manage to see your particular anguish in you. Not the anguish of being a dog which was your only possible form. But the anguish of existing so perfectly that it was becoming an unbearable joy: then you'd leap and lick my face with a freely given love and a certain threat of hatred as if I were the one who, through friendship, had exposed you. I'm pretty sure now I wasn't the one who had a dog. You were the one who had a person.

'But you possessed a person so powerful that he could

43

choose: and so he abandoned you. With relief he abandoned you. With relief, yes, since you demanded – with the serene and simple incomprehension of one who is a heroic dog – that I be a man. He abandoned you with an excuse the whole household approved of: since how could I move house with all that baggage and family, and on top of that a dog, while adjusting to a new high school and a new city, and on top of that a dog? "Who there's no room for," said Marta being practical. "Who'll bother the other passengers," reasoned my mother-in-law without knowing that I'd already thought of excuses, and the children cried, and I looked neither at them nor at you, José. But you and I alone know that I abandoned you because you were the constant possibility of the crime never committed. The possibility that I would sin which, in the concealment of my eyes, was already a sin. So I sinned right away to be guilty right away. And this crime stands in for the greater crime that I wouldn't have the nerve to commit,' thought the man ever more lucidly.

'There are so many ways to be guilty and lose yourself forever and betray yourself and not face yourself. I chose to hurt a dog,' thought the man. 'Because I knew that would be a lesser crime and that no one goes to Hell for abandoning a dog that trusted a man. Because I knew that crime wasn't punishable.'

As he sat on the plateau, his mathematical head was cool and intelligent. Only now did he seem to comprehend, in all his icy plenitude, that what he'd done to the dog was truly unpunished and everlasting. For they hadn't yet invented a punishment for the great concealed crimes and for the profound betrayals.

A man might yet outsmart the Last Judgment. No one condemned him for this crime. Not even the Church. 'They're all my accomplices, José. I'd have to go door to door and beg them to accuse me and punish me: they'd all slam the door on me with suddenly hardened faces. No one condemns me for this crime. Not even you, José, would condemn me. For all I'd have to do, powerful as I am, is decide to call you – and, emerging from your abandonment in the streets, in one leap you'd lick my cheek with joy and forgiveness. I'd turn the other cheek for you to kiss.'

The man took off his glasses, sighed, put them back on.

He looked at the covered grave. Where he had buried an unknown dog in tribute to the abandoned dog, attempting at last to repay the debt that distressingly no one was demanding. Attempting to punish himself with an act of kindness and be freed of his crime. The way someone gives alms in order at last to eat the cake for which another went without bread.

But as if José, the abandoned dog, demanded much more from him than this lie; as if he were demanding that he, in a final push, be a man – and as a man take responsibility for his crime – he looked at the grave where he had buried his weakness and his condition.

And now, more mathematically still, he sought a way

not to have punished himself. He shouldn't be consoled. He coolly sought a way to destroy the false burial of the unknown dog. He crouched then, and, solemn, calm, with simple movements – unburied the dog. The dark dog at last appeared whole, unfamiliar with dirt in its eyelashes, its eyes open and glazed over. And thus the mathematics teacher renewed his crime forever. The man then looked around and to the heavens beseeching a witness to what he had done. And as if that still weren't enough, he started descending the slopes toward the bosom of his family.

The Buffalo

But it was spring. even the lion licked the lioness's smooth forehead. Both animals blond. The woman averted her eyes from the cage, where the hot smell alone recalled the carnage she'd come looking for at the Zoological Gardens. Then the lion paced calmly, mane flowing, and the lioness slowly recomposed the head of a sphinx upon her outstretched paws. 'But this is love, it's love again,' railed the woman trying to locate her own hatred but it was spring and two lions had been in love. Fists in her coat pockets, she looked around, surrounded by the cages, caged by the shut cages. She kept walking. Her eyes were so focused on searching that her vision sometimes darkened into a kind of sleep, and then she'd recompose herself as in the coolness of a pit.

But the giraffe was a virgin with freshly shorn braids. With the mindless innocence of large and nimble and guiltless things. The woman in the brown coat averted her eyes, feeling sick, sick. Unable – in front of the perching aerial giraffe, in front of that silent wingless bird – unable to locate inside herself the spot where her sickness was the worst, the sickest spot, the spot of hatred, she who had gone to the Zoological Gardens to get sick. But not in front of the giraffe that was more landscape than being. Not in front of that flesh that had become distracted in its height and remoteness, the nearly verdant giraffe. She was searching for other animals, trying to learn from them how to hate. The hippopotamus, the moist hippopotamus. That plump roll of flesh, rounded and mute flesh awaiting some other plump and mute flesh. No. For there was such humble love in remaining just flesh, such sweet martyrdom in not knowing how to think.

But it was spring, and, tightening the fist in her coat pocket, she'd kill those monkeys levitating in their cage, monkeys happy as weeds, monkeys leaping about gently, the female monkey with her resigned, loving gaze, and the other female suckling her young. She'd kill them with fifteen dry bullets: the woman's teeth clenched until her jaw ached. The nakedness of the monkeys. The world that saw no danger in being naked. She'd kill the nakedness of the monkeys. One monkey stared back at her as he gripped the bars, his emaciated arms outstretched in a crucifix, his bare chest exposed without pride. But she wouldn't aim at his chest, she'd shoot the monkey between the eyes, she'd shoot between those eyes that were staring at her without blinking. Suddenly the woman averted her face: because the monkey's pupils were covered with a gelatinous white veil, in his eyes the sweetness of sickness, he was an old monkey – the woman averted her face, trapping between her teeth a feeling she hadn't come looking for, she quickened her step, even so, turned her head in alarm back toward the monkey with its arms outstretched: he kept staring straight ahead. 'Oh no, not this,' she thought. And as she fled, she said: 'God, teach me only how to hate.'

'I hate you,' she said to a man whose only crime was not loving her. 'I hate you,' she said in a rush. But she didn't even know how you were supposed to do it. How did you dig in the earth until locating that black water, how did you open a passage through the hard earth and never reach yourself? She roamed the zoo amid mothers and children. But the elephant withstood his own weight. That whole elephant endowed with the capacity to crush with a mere foot. But he didn't crush anything. That power that nevertheless would tamely let itself be led to a circus, a children's elephant. And his eyes, with an old man's benevolence, trapped inside that hulking, inherited flesh. The oriental elephant. And the oriental spring too, and everything being born, everything flowing downstream.

The woman then tried the camel. The camel in rags, humpbacked, chewing at himself, absorbed in the process of getting to know his food. She felt weak and tired, she'd hardly eaten in two days. The camel's large, dusty eyelashes above eyes dedicated to the patience of an internal craft. Patience, patience, patience, was all she was finding in this windblown spring. Tears filled the woman's eyes, tears that didn't spill over, trapped inside the patience of her inherited flesh. The camel's dusty odor was all that arose from this encounter she had come for: for dry hatred, not for tears. She approached the bars of the pen, inhaled the dust of that old carpet where ashen blood flowed, sought its impure tepidness, pleasure ran down her back into the distress, but still not the distress she'd come looking for. In her stomach the urge to kill convulsed in hunger pangs. But not the camel in ragged burlap. 'Dear God, who shall be my mate in this world?'

So she went alone to have her violence. In the zoo's small amusement park she waited meditatively in the line of lovers for her turn on the roller coaster.

And there she was sitting now, quiet in her brown coat. Her seat stopped for now, the roller-coaster machinery stopped for now. Separate from everyone in her seat, she looked like she was sitting in a Church. Her lowered eyes saw the ground between the tracks. The ground where simply out of love – love, love, not love! – where out of pure love weeds sprouted between the tracks in a light green so dizzying that she had to avert her eyes in tormented temptation. The breeze made the hair rise on the back of her neck, she shivered refusing it, in temptation refusing, it was always so much easier to love.

But all of a sudden came that lurch of the guts, that halting of a heart caught by surprise in midair, that fright, the triumphant fury with which her seat hurtled her into the nothing and immediately swept her up like a rag doll, skirts flying, the deep resentment with which she became mechanical, her body automatically joyful – the girl-friends' shrieks! – her gaze wounded by that enormous surprise, that offense, 'they were having their way with her,' that enormous offense – the girlfriends' shrieks! – the enormous bewilderment at finding herself spasmodically frolicking, they were having their way with her, her pure whiteness suddenly exposed. How many minutes? the minutes of an extended scream of a train rounding the bend, and the joy of another plunge through the air insulting her like a kick, her dancing erratically in the wind, dancing frantically, whether or not she wanted it her body shook like someone laughing, that sensation of laughing to death, the sudden death of someone who had neglected to shred all those papers in the drawer, not other people's death, her own, always her own. She who could have taken advantage of the others screaming to let out her own howl of lament, she forgot herself, all she felt was fright.

And now this silence, sudden too. They'd come back to earth, the machinery once again completely stopped.

Pale, kicked out of a Church, she looked at the stationary earth from which she'd departed and back to which she'd been delivered. She straightened out her skirts primly. She didn't look at anyone. Contrite as on that day when in the middle of everyone the entire contents of her purse had spilled onto the ground and everything that was valuable while lying secretly in her purse, once exposed in the dust of the street, revealed the pettiness of a private life of precautions: face powder, receipt, fountain pen, her retrieving from the curb the scaffolding of her life. She rose from her seat stunned as if shaking off a collision. Though no one was paying attention, she smoothed her skirt again, did what she could so no one would notice how weak and disgraced she was, haughtily protecting her broken bones. But the sky was spinning in her empty stomach; the earth, rising and falling before her eyes, remained distant for a few moments, the earth that is always so troublesome. For a moment the woman wanted, in mutely sobbing fatigue, to reach out her hand to the troublesome earth: her hand reached out like that of a crippled beggar. But as if she had swallowed the void, her heart stunned.

Was that it? That was it. Of the violence, that was it.

She headed back toward the animals. The ordeal of the roller coaster had left her subdued. She didn't make it much further: she had to rest her forehead against the bars of a cage, exhausted, her breath coming quick and shallow. From inside the cage the coati looked at her. She looked at him. Not a single word exchanged. She could never hate that coati who looked at her with the silence of an inquiring body. Disturbed, she averted her eyes from the coati's simplicity. The curious coati asking her a question the way a child asks. And she averting her eyes, concealing from him her deadly mission. Her forehead was pressed against the bars so firmly that for an instant it looked like she was the caged one and a free coati was examining her.

The cage was always on the side she was: she let out a moan that seemed to come from the soles of her feet. After that another moan.

Then, born from her womb, it rose again, beseeching, in a swelling wave, that urge to kill – her eyes welled up grateful and black in a near-happiness, it wasn't hatred yet, for the time being just the tormented urge to hate like a desire, the promise of cruel blossoming, a torment like love, the urge to hate promising itself sacred blood and triumph, the spurned female had become spiritualized through her great hope. But where, where to find the animal that would teach her to have her own hatred? the hatred that was hers by right but that lay excruciatingly out of reach? where could she learn to hate so as not to die of love? And from whom? The world of spring, the world of beasts that in spring Christianize themselves with paws that claw but do not wound . . . oh no more of this world! no more of this perfume, of this weary panting, no more of this forgiveness in everything that will die one day as if made to surrender. Never forgiveness, if that woman forgave one more time, even just once, her life would be lost – she let out a hoarse, brief moan, the coati gave a start – caged in she looked around, and since she wasn't the kind of person people paid attention to, she crouched down like an old solitary assassin, a child ran past without noticing her.

Then she started walking again, smaller now, tough, fists once again braced in her pockets, the undercover assassin, and everything was caught in her chest. In her chest that knew only how to give up, knew only how to withstand, knew only how to beg forgiveness, knew only how to forgive, that had only learned how to have the sweetness of unhappiness, and learned only how to love, love, love. Imagining that she might never experience the hatred of which her forgiveness had always been made, this caused her heart to moan indecently, she began walking so fast that she seemed to have found a sudden destiny. She was almost running, her shoes throwing her off balance, and giving her a physical fragility that once again reduced her to the imprisoned female, her steps mechanically assumed the beseeching despair of the frail, she who was nothing more than a frail woman herself. But, if she could take off her shoes, could she avoid the joy of walking barefoot? how could you not love the ground on which you walk? She moaned again, stopped before the bars of an enclosure, pressed her hot face against the iron's rusty coolness. Eyes deeply shut she tried to bury her face between the hardness of the railings, her face attempted an impossible passage through the narrow bars, just as before when she'd seen the newborn monkey seek in the blindness of hunger the female's breast. A fleeting comfort came from how the bars seemed to hate her while opposing her with the resistance of frozen iron.

She opened her eyes slowly. Her eyes coming from

their own darkness couldn't see a thing in the afternoon's faint light. She stood there breathing. Gradually she started to make things out again, gradually shapes began solidifying, she was tired, crushed by the sweetness of tiredness. Her head tilted inquiringly toward the budding trees, her eyes saw the small white clouds. Without hope, she heard the lightness of a stream. She lowered her head again and stood gazing at the buffalo in the distance. Inside in a brown coat, breathing without interest, no one interested in her, she interested in no one.

A certain peace at last. The breeze ruffling the hair on her forehead as if brushing the hair of someone who had just died, whose forehead was still damp with sweat. Gazing detachedly at that great dry plot surrounded by tall railings, the buffalo plot. The black buffalo was standing still at the far end of that plot. Then he paced in the distance on his narrow haunches, his dense haunches. His neck thicker than his tensed flanks. Seen straight on, his large head was broader than his body, blocking the rest from view, like a severed head. And on his head those horns. At a distance he slowly paced with his torso. He was a black buffalo. So black that from afar his face looked featureless. Atop his blackness the erect stark whiteness of his horns.

The woman might have left but the silence felt good in the waning afternoon.

And in the silence of the paddock, those meandering steps, the dry dust beneath those dry hooves. At a distance, in the midst of his calm pacing, the black buffalo looked at her for an instant. The next instant, the woman again saw only the hard muscle of his body. Maybe he hadn't looked at her. She couldn't tell, since all she could discern of that shadowy head were its outlines. But once more he seemed to have either seen or sensed her.

The woman raised her head a little, retracted it slightly in misgiving. Body motionless, head back, she waited.

And once more the buffalo seemed to notice her.

As if she couldn't stand feeling what she had felt, she suddenly averted her face and looked at a tree. Her heart didn't beat in her chest, her heart was beating hollowly somewhere between her stomach and intestines.

The buffalo made another slow loop. The dust. The woman clenched her teeth, her whole face ached a little.

The buffalo with his constricted torso. In the luminous dusk he was a body blackened with tranquil rage, the woman sighed slowly. A white thing had spread out inside her, white as paper, fragile as paper, intense as a whiteness. Death droned in her ears. The buffalo's renewed pacing brought her back to herself and, with another long sigh, she returned to the surface. She didn't know where she'd been. She was standing, very feeble, just emerged from that white and remote thing where she'd been.

And from where she looked back at the buffalo.

The buffalo larger now. The black buffalo. Ah, she said suddenly with a pang. The buffalo with his back turned to her, standing still. The woman's whitened face didn't know how to call him. Ah! she said provoking him. Ah! she said. Her face was covered in deathly whiteness, her suddenly gaunt face held purity and veneration. Ah! she goaded him through clenched teeth. But with his back turned, the buffalo completely still.

She picked up a rock off the ground and hurled it into the paddock. The torso's stillness, quieted down even blacker: the rock rolled away uselessly.

Ah! she said shaking the bars. That white thing was spreading inside her, viscous like a kind of saliva. The buffalo with his back turned.

Ah, she said. But this time because inside her at last was flowing a first trickle of black blood.

The first instant was one of pain. As if the world had convulsed for this blood to flow. She stood there, listening to that first bitter oil drip as in a grotto, the spurned female. Her strength was still trapped between the bars, but something incomprehensible and burning, ultimately incomprehensible, was happening, a thing like a joy tasted in her mouth. Then the buffalo turned toward her.

The buffalo turned, stood still, and faced her from afar.

I love you, she then said with hatred to the man whose great unpunishable crime was not wanting her. I hate you, she said beseeching the buffalo's love.

Provoked at last, the enormous buffalo approached unhurriedly.

He approached, the dust rose. The woman waited with her arms hanging alongside her coat. Slowly he approached. She didn't take a single step back. Until he reached the railings and stopped there. There stood the buffalo and the woman, face to face. She didn't look at his face, or his mouth, or his horns. She looked him in the eye.

And the buffalo's eyes, his eyes looked her in the eye. And such a deep pallor was exchanged that the woman fell into a drowsy torpor. Standing, in a deep sleep. Small red eyes were looking at her. The eyes of the buffalo. The woman was dazed in surprise, slowly shaking her head. The calm buffalo. Slowly the woman was shaking her head, astonished by the hatred with which the buffalo, tranquil with hatred, was looking at her. Nearly absolved, shaking an incredulous head, her mouth slightly open. Innocent, curious, plunging deeper and deeper into those eyes staring unhurriedly at her, simple, with a drowsy sigh, neither wanting nor able to flee, trapped in this mutual murder. Trapped as if her hand were forever stuck to the dagger she herself had thrust. Trapped, as she slid spellbound down the railing. In such slow dizziness that just before her body gently crumpled the woman saw the whole sky and a buffalo.

The Egg and the Chicken

In the morning in the kitchen on the table I see the egg.

I look at the egg with a single gaze. Immediately I perceive that one cannot be seeing an egg. Seeing an egg never remains in the present: as soon as I see an egg it already becomes having seen an egg three millennia ago. – At the very instant of seeing the egg it is the memory of an egg. – The egg can only be seen by one who has already seen it. – When one sees the egg it is too late: an egg seen is an egg lost. – Seeing the egg is the promise of one day eventually seeing the egg. – A brief and indivisible glance; if indeed there is thought; there is none; there is the egg. – Looking is the necessary instrument that, once used, I shall discard. I shall keep the egg. – The egg has no itself. Individually it does not exist.

Seeing the egg is impossible: the egg is supervisible just as there are supersonic sounds. No one can see the egg. Does the dog see the egg? Only machines see the egg. The construction crane sees the egg. – When I was ancient an egg landed on my shoulder. – Love for the egg cannot be felt either. Love for the egg is supersensible. We do not know that we love the egg. – When I was ancient I was keeper of the egg and I would tread lightly to avoid upending the egg's silence. When I died, they removed the egg from me with care. It was still alive. – Only one who saw the world would see the egg. Like the world, the egg is obvious.

The egg no longer exists. Like the light of an already-dead star, the egg properly speaking no longer exists. – You are perfect, egg. You are white. – To you I dedicate the beginning. To you I dedicate the first time.

To the egg I dedicate the Chinese nation.

The egg is a suspended thing. It has never landed. When it lands, it is not what has landed. It was a thing under the egg. – I look at the egg in the kitchen with superficial attention so as not to break it. I take the utmost care not to understand it. Since it is impossible to understand, I know that if I understand it this is because I am making an error. Understanding is the proof of making an error. Understanding it is not the way to see it. – Never thinking about the egg is a way to have seen it. – I wonder, do I know of the egg? I almost certainly do. Thus: I exist, therefore I know. – What I don't know about the egg is what really matters. What I don't know about the egg gives me the egg properly speaking. – The Moon is inhabited by eggs.

The egg is an exteriorization. To have a shell is to surrender. – The egg denudes the kitchen. It turns the table into a slanted plane. The egg exposes. – Whoever plunges deeper into an egg, whoever sees more than the surface of the egg, is after something else: that person is hungry.

An egg is the soul of the chicken. The awkward chicken. The sure egg. The frightened chicken. The sure egg. Like a paused projectile. For an egg is an egg in space. An egg upon blue. – I love you, egg. I love you as a thing doesn't even know it loves another thing. – I do not touch it. The aura of my fingers is what sees the egg. I do not touch it. – But to dedicate myself to the vision of the egg would be to die to the world, and I need the yolk and the white. – The egg sees me. Does the egg idealize me? Does the egg meditate me? No, the egg merely sees me. It is exempt from the understanding that wounds. – The egg has never struggled. It is a gift. – The egg is invisible to the naked eye. From one egg to another one arrives at God, who is invisible to the naked eye. – The egg could have been a triangle that rolled for so long in space that it became oval. – Is the egg basically a vessel? Could it have been the first vessel sculpted by the Etruscans? No. The egg originated in Macedonia. There it was calculated, fruit of the most arduous spontaneity. In the sands of Macedonia a man holding a stick drew it. And then erased it with his bare foot.

An egg is a thing that must be careful. That's why the chicken is the egg's disguise. The chicken exists so that the egg can traverse the ages. That's what a mother is for. – The egg is constantly persecuted for being too ahead of its time. – An egg, for now, will always be revolutionary. – It lives inside the chicken to avoid being called white. The egg really is white. But it cannot be called white. Not because that harms it, but people who call the egg white, those people die to life. Calling something white that is white can destroy humanity. Once a man was accused of being what he was, and he was called That Man. They weren't lying: He was. But to this day we still haven't recovered, one after the next. The general law for us to stay alive: one can say 'a pretty face,' but whoever says 'the face,' dies; for having exhausted the topic.

Over time, the egg became a chicken egg. It is not. But, once it was adopted, it took that name. – One should say 'the chicken's egg.' If one merely says 'the egg,' the topic is exhausted, and the world becomes naked. – When it comes to the egg, the danger lies in discovering what might be called beauty, that is, its veracity. The veracity of the egg is not verisimilar. If they find out, they might want to force it to become rectangular. The danger is not for the egg, it wouldn't become rectangular. (Our guarantee is that it is unable: being unable is the egg's great strength: its grandiosity comes from the greatness of being unable, which radiates from it like a not-wanting.) But whoever struggles to make it rectangular would be losing his own life. The egg puts us, therefore, in danger. Our advantage is that the egg is invisible. And as for the initiates, the initiates disguise the egg.

As for the chicken's body, the chicken's body is the greatest proof that the egg does not exist. All you have to do is look at the chicken to make it obvious that the egg cannot possibly exist.

And what about the chicken? The egg is the chicken's great sacrifice. The egg is the cross the chicken bears in life. The egg is the chicken's unattainable dream. The chicken loves the egg. She doesn't know the egg exists. If she knew she had an egg inside her, would she save herself? If she knew she had the egg inside her, she would lose her state of being a chicken. Being a chicken is the chicken's survival. Surviving is salvation. For living doesn't seem to exist. Living leads to death. So what the chicken does is be permanently surviving. Surviving is what's called keeping up the struggle against life that is deadly. That's what being a chicken is. The chicken looks embarrassed.

The chicken must not know she has an egg. Or else she would save herself as a chicken, which is no guarantee either, but she would lose the egg. So she doesn't know. The chicken exists so that the egg can use the chicken. She was only meant to be fulfilled, but she liked it. The chicken's undoing comes from this: liking wasn't part of being born. To like being alive hurts. – As for which came first, it was the egg that found the chicken. The chicken was not even summoned. The chicken is directly singled out. – The chicken lives as if in a dream. She has no sense of reality. All the chicken's fright comes because they're always interrupting her reverie. The chicken is a sound sleep. – The chicken suffers from an unknown ailment.

The chicken's unknown ailment is the egg. – She doesn't know how to explain herself: 'I know that the error is inside me,' she calls her life an error, 'I don't know what I feel anymore,' etc.

'Etc., etc., etc.,' is what the chicken clucks all day long. The chicken has plenty of inner life. To be honest, the only thing the chicken really has is inner life. Our vision of her inner life is what we call 'chicken.' The chicken's inner life consists of acting as if she understands. At the slightest threat she screams bloody murder like a maniac. All this so the egg won't break inside her. An egg that breaks inside the chicken is like blood.

The chicken looks at the horizon. As if it were from the line of the horizon that an egg is coming. Beyond being a mode of transport for the egg, the chicken is silly, idle and myopic. How could the chicken understand herself if she is the contradiction of an egg? The egg is still the same one that originated in Macedonia. The chicken is always the most modern of tragedies. She is always pointlessly current. And she keeps being redrawn. The most suitable form for a chicken has yet to be found. While my neighbor talks on the phone he redraws the chicken with an absentminded pencil. But there's nothing to be done for the chicken: part of her nature is not to be of use to herself. Given, however, that her destiny is more important than she is, and given that her destiny is the egg, her personal life does not concern us.

Inside herself the chicken doesn't recognize the egg,

but neither does she recognize it outside herself. When the chicken sees the egg she thinks she's dealing with something impossible. And with her heart beating, with her heart beating so, she doesn't recognize it.

Suddenly I look at the egg in the kitchen and all I see in it is food. I don't recognize it, and my heart beats. The metamorphosis is happening inside me: I start not to be able to discern the egg anymore. Beyond every particular egg, beyond every egg that's eaten, the egg does not exist. I can now no longer believe in an egg. More and more I lack the strength to believe, I am dying, farewell, I looked at an egg too long and it started putting me to sleep.

The chicken who didn't want to sacrifice her life. The one who chose wanting to be 'happy.' The one who didn't notice that, if she spent her life designing the egg inside herself as in an illuminated manuscript, she would be good for something. The one who didn't know how to lose herself. The one who thought she had chicken feathers to cover her because she had precious skin, not understanding that the feathers were meant exclusively for helping her along as she carried the egg, because intense suffering might harm the egg. The one who thought pleasure was a gift to her, not realizing that it was meant to keep her completely distracted while the egg was being formed. The one who didn't know 'I' is just one of those words you draw while talking on the phone, a mere attempt to find a better shape. The one who thought 'I' means having a oneself. The chickens who harm the egg are those that are a ceaseless 'I.' In them, the 'I' is so constant that they can no longer utter the word 'egg.' But, who knows, maybe that's exactly what the egg was in need of. For if they weren't so distracted, if they paid attention to the great life forming inside them, they would get in the way of the egg.

I started talking about the chicken and for a while now I have no longer been talking about the chicken. But I'm still talking about the egg.

And thus I don't understand the egg. I only understand a broken egg: I crack it on the frying pan. In this indirect way I give myself to the egg's existence: my sacrifice is reducing myself to my personal life. I turned my pleasure and my pain into my hidden destiny. And having only one's own life is, for those who have already seen the egg, a sacrifice. Like the ones who, in a convent, sweep the floor and do the laundry, serving without the glory of a higher purpose, my job is to live out my pleasures and my pains. I must have the modesty to live.

I pick up another egg in the kitchen, I break its shell and shape. And from this precise moment there was never an egg. It is absolutely essential that I be a busy and distracted person. I am necessarily one of those people who refuse. I belong to that Masonic society of those who once saw the egg and refused it as a way to protect it. We are the ones who abstain from destroying, and by doing so are consumed. We, undercover agents dispersed among less revealing duties, we sometimes recognize each other.

By a certain way of looking, by a way of shaking hands, we recognize each other and call this love. And then our disguise is unnecessary: though we don't speak, neither do we lie, though we don't speak the truth, neither must we dissemble any longer. Love is when we are allowed to participate a bit more. Few want love, because love is the great disillusionment with all the rest. And few can bear losing the rest of their illusions. There are people who would volunteer for love, thinking love will enrich their personal lives. On the contrary: love is ultimately poverty. Love is not having. Moreover love is the disillusionment of what you thought was love. And it's no prize, that's why it doesn't make people vain, love is no prize, it's a status granted exclusively to people who, without it, would defile the egg with their personal suffering. That doesn't make love an honorable exception; it is granted precisely to those bad agents, those who would ruin everything if they weren't allowed to guess at things vaguely.

All the agents are granted several advantages so that the egg may form. It is no cause for envy since, even certain statuses, worse than other people's, are merely the ideal conditions for the egg. As for the agents' pleasure, they also receive it without pride. They austerely experience all pleasures: it is even our sacrifice so that the egg may form. Upon us has been imposed, as well, a nature entirely prone to much pleasure. Which makes it easier. At the very least it makes pleasure less arduous.

There are cases of agents committing suicide: they find

the minimal instructions they have received insufficient, and feel unsupported. There was the case of the agent who publicly revealed himself as an agent because he found not being understood intolerable, and could no longer stand not being respected by others: he was fatally run over as he was leaving a restaurant. There was another who didn't even have to be eliminated: he was slowly consumed by his own rebellion, his rebellion came when he discovered that the two or three instructions he had received included no explanation whatsoever. There was another, eliminated too, because he thought 'the truth should be bravely spoken,' and started first of all to seek it out; they say he died in the name of the truth, but in fact he was just making the truth harder with his innocence; his seeming bravery was foolhardiness, and his desire for loyalty was naive, he hadn't understood that being loyal isn't so tidy, being loyal means being disloyal to everything else. Those extreme cases of death aren't caused by cruelty. It's because there's a job, let's call it cosmic, to be done, and individual cases unfortunately cannot be taken into consideration. For those who succumb and become individuals there are institutions, charity, comprehension that doesn't distinguish motives, in a word our human life.

The eggs crackle in the frying pan, and lost in a dream I make breakfast. Lacking any sense of reality, I shout for the children who sprout from various beds, drag the chairs out and eat, and the work of the breaking day begins, shouted and laughed and eaten, white and yolk, merriment amid fighting, the day that is our salt and we are the day's salt, living is extremely tolerable, living keeps us busy and distracts us, living makes us laugh.

And it makes me smile in my mystery. My mystery is that being merely a means, and not an end, has given me the most mischievous of freedoms: I'm no fool and I make the most of things. Even to the point of wronging others so much that, frankly. The fake job they have given me to disguise my true purpose, since I make the most of this fake job and turn it into my real one; this includes the money they give me as a daily allowance to ease my life so that the egg may form, since I have used this money for other purposes, diverting the funds, I recently bought stock in Brahma beer and am rich. All this I still call having the necessary modesty to live. And also the time they have granted me, and that they grant us just so that in this honorable leisure the egg may form, well I have used this time for illicit pleasures and illicit pains, completely forgetting the egg. That is my simplicity.

Or is that exactly what they want to happen to me, precisely so the egg can carry out its mission? Is it freedom or am I being controlled? Because I keep noticing how every error of mine has been put to use. My rebellion is that for them I am nothing, I am merely valuable: they take care of me from one second to the next, with the most absolute lack of love; I am merely valuable. With the money they give me, I have taken to drinking lately. Abuse of trust? But it's because nobody knows how it feels inside for someone whose job consists of pretending that she is betraying, and who ends up believing in her own betrayal. Whose job consists of forgetting every day. Someone of whom apparent dishonor is required. Not even my mirror still reflects a face that is mine. Either I am an agent, or it really is betrayal.

Yet I sleep the sleep of the righteous because I know that my futile life doesn't interfere with the march of great time. On the contrary: it seems that I am required to be extremely futile, I'm even required to sleep like one of the righteous. They want me busy and distracted, and they don't care how. Because, with my misguided attention and grave foolishness, I could interfere with whatever is carried out through me. It's because I myself, I properly speaking, all I have really been good for is interfering. What tells me that I might be an agent is the idea that my destiny surpasses me: at least they really did have to let me guess that, I was one of those people who would do their job badly if they couldn't guess at least a little; they made me forget what they had let me guess, but I still had the vague notion that my destiny surpasses me, and that I am an instrument of their work. But in any case all I could be was an instrument, since the work couldn't really be mine. I have already tried to set myself up on my own and it didn't work out; my hand trembles to this day. Had I kept at it any longer I would have damaged my health forever. Since then, ever since that thwarted experiment, I have tried to consider things this way: that much has already been given me, that they have granted me everything that might be granted; and that other agents, far superior to me, have also worked solely for something they did not know. And with the same minimal instructions. Much has already been given me; this, for example: every once in a while, with my heart beating at the privilege, I at least know that I am not recognizing anything! with my heart beating from emotion, I at least do not understand! with my heart beating from trust, I at least do not know.

But what about the egg? This is one of their ploys: while I was talking about the egg, I had forgotten the egg. 'Talk, talk!' they instructed me. And the egg is fully protected by all those words. Keep talking, is one of the instructions, I am so tired.

Out of devotion to the egg, I forgot it. My necessary forgetting. My self-serving forgetting. Because the egg is an evasion. In the face of my possessive adoration it could retreat and never again return. But if it is forgotten. If I make the sacrifice of living only my life and of forgetting it. If the egg becomes impossible. Then – free, delicate, with no message for me – perhaps one last time it will move from space over to this window that I have always left open. And at dawn it will descend into our building. Serene all the way to the kitchen. Illuminating it with my pallor.

Mineirinho

Yes, I suppose it is in myself, as one of the representatives of us, that I should seek the reasons why the death of a thug is hurting. And why it does me more good to count the thirteen gunshots that killed Mineirinho rather than his crimes. I asked my cook what she thought about it. I saw in her face the slight convulsion of a conflict, the distress of not understanding what one feels, of having to betray contradictory feelings because one cannot reconcile them. Indisputable facts, but indisputable revolt as well, the violent compassion of revolt. Feeling divided by one's own confusion about being unable to forget that Mineirinho was dangerous and had already killed too many; and still we wanted him to live. The cook grew slightly guarded, seeing me perhaps as an avenging justice. Somewhat angry at me, who was prying into her soul, she answered coldly: 'It's no use saying what I feel. Who doesn't know Mineirinho was a criminal? But I'm sure he was saved and is already in heaven.' I answered, 'More than lots of people who haven't killed anyone.'

Why? For the first law, the one that protects the irreplaceable body and life, is thou shalt not kill. It is my greatest assurance: that way they won't kill me, because I don't want to die, and that way they won't let me kill, because having killed would be darkness for me.

This is the law. But there is something that, if it makes me hear the first and the second gunshots with the relief of safety, at the third puts me on the alert, at the fourth unsettles me, the fifth and the sixth cover me in shame, the seventh and eighth I hear with my heart pounding in horror, at the ninth and tenth my mouth is quivering, at the eleventh I say God's name in fright, at the twelfth I call my brother. The thirteenth shot murders me – because I am the other. Because I want to be the other.

That justice that watches over my sleep, I repudiate it, humiliated that I need it. Meanwhile I sleep and falsely save myself. We, the essential phonies. For my house to function, I demand as my primary duty that I be a phony, that I not exercise my revolt and my love, both set aside. If I am not a phony, my house trembles. I must have forgotten that beneath the house is the land, the ground upon which a new house might be erected. Meanwhile we sleep and falsely save ourselves. Until thirteen gunshots wake us up, and in horror I plead too late – twenty-eight years after Mineirinho was born – that in killing this cornered man, they do not kill him in us. Because I know that he is my error. And out of a whole lifetime, by God, sometimes the only thing that saves a person is error, and I know that we shall not be saved so long as our error is not precious to us. My error is my mirror, where I see what

73

in silence I made of a man. My error is the way I saw life opening up in his flesh and I was aghast, and I saw the substance of life, placenta and blood, the living mud. In Mineirinho my way of living burst. How could I not love him, if he lived up till the thirteenth gunshot the very thing that I had been sleeping? His frightened violence. His innocent violence – not in its consequences, but innocent in itself as that of a son whose father neglected him. Everything that was violence in him is furtive in us, and we avoid each other's gaze so as not to run the risk of understanding each other. So that the house won't tremble. The violence bursting in Mineirinho that only another man's hand, the hand of hope, resting on his stunned and wounded head, could appease and make his startled eyes lift and at last fill with tears. Only after a man is found inert on the ground, without his cap or shoes, do I see that I forgot to tell him: me too.

I don't want this house. I want a justice that would have given a chance to something pure and full of help-lessness in Mineirinho – that thing that moves mountains and is the same as what made him love a woman 'like a madman,' and the same that led him through a doorway so narrow that it slashes into nakedness; it is a thing in us as intense and transparent as a dangerous gram of radium, that thing is a grain of life that if trampled is transformed into something threatening – into trampled love; that thing, which in Mineirinho became a knife, it is the same thing in me that makes me offer another man water, not because I have water, but because, I too, know what thirst is; and I too, who have not lost my way, have experienced perdition. Prior justice, that would not make me ashamed. It was past time for us, with or without irony, to be more divine; if we can guess what God's benevolence might be it is because we guess at benevolence in ourselves, whatever sees the man before he succumbs to the sickness of crime. I go on, nevertheless, waiting for God to be the father, when I know that one man can be father to another. And I go on living in my weak house. That house, whose protective door I lock so tightly, that house won't withstand the first gale that will send a locked door flying through the air. But it is standing, and Mineirinho lived rage on my behalf, while I was calm. He was gunned down in his disoriented strength, while a god fabricated at the last second hastily blesses my composed wrongdoing and my stupefied justice: what upholds the walls of my house is the certainty that I shall always vindicate myself, my friends won't vindicate me, but my enemies who are my accomplices, they will greet me; what upholds me is knowing that I shall always fabricate a god in the image of whatever I need in order to sleep peacefully, and that others will furtively pretend that we are all in the right and that there is nothing to be done. All this, yes, for we are the essential phonies, bastions of some thing. And above all trying not to understand.

Because the one who understands disrupts. There is something in us that would disrupt everything – a thing that understands. That thing that stays silent before the man without his cap or shoes, and to get them he robbed and killed; and stays silent before Saint George of gold and diamonds. That very serious thing in me grows more serious still when faced with the man felled by machine guns. Is that thing the killer inside me? No, it is the despair inside us. Like madmen, we know him, that dead man in whom the gram of radium caught fire. But only like madmen, and not phonies, do we know him. It is as a madman that I enter a life that so often has no doorway, and as a madman that I comprehend things dangerous to comprehend, and only as a madman do I feel deep love, that is confirmed when I see that the radium will radiate regardless, if not through trust, hope and love, then miserably through the sick courage of destruction. If I weren't mad, I'd be eight hundred policemen with eight hundred machine guns, and this would be my honorableness.

Until a slightly madder justice came along. One that would take into account that we all must speak for a man driven to despair because in him human speech has already failed, he is already so mute that only a brute incoherent cry serves as signal. A prior justice that would recall how our great struggle is that of fear, and that a man who kills many does so because he was very much afraid. Above all a justice that would examine itself, and see that all of us, living mud, are dark, and that is why not even one man's wrongdoing can be surrendered to another man's wrongdoing: so that this other man cannot commit, freely and with approbation, the crime of gunning someone down. A justice that does not forget that we are all dangerous, and that the moment that the deliverer of justice kills, he is no longer protecting us or trying to eliminate a criminal, he is committing his own personal crime, one long held inside him. At the moment he kills a criminal – in that instant an innocent is killed. No, it's not that I want the sublime, nor for things to turn into words to make me sleep peacefully, a combination of forgiveness, of vague charity, we who seek shelter in the abstract.

What I want is much rougher and more difficult: I want the land.

Covert Joy

She was fat, short, freckled, and had reddish, excessively frizzy hair. She had a huge bust, while the rest of us were still flat-chested. As if that weren't enough, she'd fill both pockets of her blouse, over her bust, with candy. But she had what any child devourer of stories would wish for: a father who owned a bookstore.

She didn't take much advantage of it. And we even less: even for birthdays, instead of at least a cheap little book, she'd present us with a postcard from her father's shop. Even worse, it would be a view of Recife itself, where we lived, with the bridges we'd seen countless times. On the back she'd write in elaborately curlicued script words like 'birthday' and 'thinking of you.'

But what a talent she had for cruelty. She was pure vengeance, sucking noisily on her candy. How that girl must have hated us, we who were unforgivably pretty, slender, tall, with flowing hair. She performed her sadism on me with calm ferocity. In my eagerness to read, I didn't even notice the humiliations to which she subjected me: I kept begging her to lend me the books she wasn't reading.

Until the momentous day came for her to start per-
forming a kind of Chinese torture on me. As if in passing,
she informed me that she owned *The Shenanigans of Little
Miss Snub-Nose*, by Monteiro Lobato.

It was a thick book, my God, it was a book you could
live with, eating it, sleeping it. And completely beyond
my means. She told me to stop by her house the next day
and she'd lend it to me.

Up until the next day I was transformed into the very
hope of joy itself: I wasn't living, I was swimming slowly
in a gentle sea, the waves carrying me to and fro.

The next day I went to her house, literally running.
She didn't live above a shop like me, but rather in a whole
house. She didn't ask me in. Looking me right in the eye,
she said she'd lent the book to another girl, and that I
should come back the next day. Mouth agape, I left
slowly, but soon enough hope completely took over again
and I started back down the street skipping, which was
my strange way of moving through the streets of Recife.
This time I didn't even fall: the promise of the book
guided me, the next day would come, the next days would
later become the rest of my life, love for the world awaited
me, I went skipping through the streets as usual and
didn't fall once.

But things didn't simply end there. The secret plan of
the bookseller's daughter was serene and diabolical. The
next day, there I stood at her front door, with a smile and
my heart beating. Only to hear her calm reply: the book

hadn't been returned yet, and I should come back the next day. Little did I know how later on, over the course of my life, the drama of 'the next day' with her would repeat itself with my heart beating.

And so it went. For how long? I don't know. She knew it would be for an indefinite time, until the bile oozed completely out of her thick body. I had already started to guess that she'd chosen me to suffer, sometimes I guess things. But, in actually guessing things, I sometimes accept them: as if whoever wants to make me suffer damn well needs me to.

For how long? I'd go to her house daily, without missing a single day. Sometimes she'd say: well I had the book yesterday afternoon, but you didn't come till this morning, so I lent it to another girl. And I, who didn't usually get dark circles under my eyes, felt those dark circles deepening under my astonished eyes.

Until one day, when I was at her front door, listening humbly and silently to her refusal, her mother appeared. She must have been wondering about the mute, daily appearance of that girl at her front door. She asked us to explain. There was a silent commotion, interrupted by words that didn't clarify much. The lady found it increasingly strange that she wasn't understanding. Until that good mother understood. She turned to her daughter and with enormous surprise exclaimed: But that book never left the house and you didn't even want to read it!

And the worst thing for that woman wasn't realizing

what was going on. It must have been the horrified realization of the kind of daughter she had. She eyed us in silence: the power of perversity in the daughter she didn't know and the little blond girl standing at the door, exhausted, out in the wind of the streets of Recife. That was when, finally regaining her composure, she said to her daughter firmly and calmly: you're going to lend that book right this minute. And to me: 'And you can keep that book for as long as you like.' Do you understand? It was worth more than giving me the book: 'for as long as I liked' is all that a person, big or small, could ever dare wish for.

How can I explain what happened next? I was stunned, and just like that the book was in my hand. I don't think I said a thing. I took the book. No, I didn't go skipping off as usual. I walked away very slowly. I know that I was holding the thick book with both hands, clutching it against my chest. As for how long it took to get home, that doesn't really matter either. My chest was hot, my heart thoughtful.

When I got home, I didn't start reading. I pretended not to have it, just so later on I could feel the shock of having it. Hours later I opened it, read a few wondrous lines, closed it again, wandered around the house, stalled even more by eating some bread and butter, pretended not to know where I had put the book, found it, opened it for a few seconds. I kept inventing the most contrived obstacles for that covert thing that was joy.

81

Joy would always be covert for mc. I must have already sensed it. Oh how I took my time! I was living in the clouds . . . There was pride and shame inside me. I was a delicate queen.

Sometimes I'd sit in the hammock, swinging with the book open on my lap, not touching it, in the purest ecstasy.

I was no longer a girl with a book: I was a woman with her lover.

In Search of a Dignity

Senhora Jorge B. Xavier simply couldn't say how she had come in. It hadn't been through a main gate. It seemed to her in a vaguely dreamy way that she had come in through some kind of narrow opening amid the rubble of a construction site, as if she'd slipped sideways through a hole made just for her. The fact is, by the time she noticed she was already inside.

And by the time she noticed, she realized that she was deep, deep inside. She was walking interminably through the underground tunnels of Maracanã Stadium or at least they seemed to her narrow caves that ended in closed rooms and when the rooms were opened they had just a single window facing the stadium. Which, at that scorchingly deserted hour, was shimmering in the extreme glare of an uncommon heat that was descending on that midwinter day.

Then the old woman went down a shadowy passage. It led her like the others to an even darker one. The tunnel ceilings seemed low to her.

And then that passage led to another that led in turn to another.

She went down the deserted passage. And then bumped into another corner. That led her to another passage that opened onto another corner.

So she kept automatically heading down passages that kept ending in other passages. Where could the classroom for the first session be? Because that's where she would find the people she'd planned to meet. The lecture might have already started. She was going to miss it, she who made every effort not to miss anything *cultural* because that's how she stayed young inside, though even from the outside no one ever guessed she was almost 70 years old, everyone assumed she was around 57.

But now, lost in the dark, inner twists and turns of Maracanã, the woman was now dragging the heavy feet of an old lady.

That's when suddenly in a passage she came upon a man who popped up out of nowhere and asked him about the lecture which the man said he knew nothing about. But that man asked a second man who had also popped suddenly from around the bend in the passage.

Then this second man told them he had seen, near the right-hand bleachers, out there in the stadium, 'two ladies and a gentleman, one of the ladies in red.' Senhora Xavier doubted these people were the group she was supposed to meet before the lecture, and in fact had already lost track of the reason she was walking around with no end in sight. In any case she followed the man out to the stadium, where she stopped, dazzled in the hollow space filled with broad daylight and open muteness, the naked stadium disemboweled, with neither ball nor match. Above all with no crowd. There was a crowd that existed through the void of its absolute absence.

Had the two ladies and gentleman already vanished down some passage?

Then the man declared with exaggerated defiance: 'Well I'm going to search for you, ma'am, and I'll find those people no matter what, they can't have vanished into thin air.'

And in fact from faraway they both spotted them. But a second later they disappeared again. It was like a child's game in which muffled peals of laughter were mocking Senhora Jorge B. Xavier.

Then she accompanied the man down further passages. Then this man too vanished around a corner.

The woman had already given up on the lecture which deep down didn't really matter to her. As long as she made it out of that tangle of endless paths. Wasn't there an exit? Then she felt like she was in an elevator stuck between floors. Wasn't there an exit?

And that's when she suddenly recalled the wording of her friend's directions on the phone: 'it's more or less near Maracanã Stadium.' In light of this memory she understood her mistake, made by a scatterbrained and distracted person who only heard half of things, the other half remaining submerged. Senhora Xavier was very inattentive. So, then, the meeting wasn't at Maracanã after all, it was just nearby. Yet that little destiny of hers had wanted her to be lost in the labyrinth.

All right, then the struggle started up again even worse: she was determined to get out and didn't know how or where. And again that man showed up in the passage who was searching for those people and who again assured her that he'd find them because they couldn't have vanished into thin air. That's exactly what he said:

'Those people can't have vanished into thin air!'

The woman informed him:

'You don't have to take the trouble to look for them, all right? Thank you very much, all right? Because the place I'm supposed to meet those people isn't in Maracanã.'

The man halted immediately to look at her in bewilderment:

'So what exactly are you doing here, ma'am?'

She wanted to explain that her life was just like that, but since she didn't even know what she meant by 'just like that' or even by 'her life,' she said nothing in reply. The man pressed the question, somewhere between suspicious and cautious: what exactly was she doing there? Nothing, the woman replied only in her mind, by that point about to collapse from exhaustion. But she didn't reply, she let him think she was crazy. Besides, she never explained herself. She knew the man decided she was crazy – and who ever said she wasn't? because didn't she feel that thing she called 'that' out of shame? Even if she knew her so-called mental health was every bit as sound as her physical health. Physical health now failing because she'd been dragging her feet for years and years walking through that labyrinth. Her via crucis. She was dressed in very heavy wool and was stifled sweating in the unexpected heat that belonged to the peak of summer, that summer day that was a freak occurrence in winter. Her legs were aching, aching under the weight of that old cross. She'd already resigned herself in a way to never making it out of Maracanã and dying there from a heart bled dry.

Then, and as always, it was only after she had given up on the things she desired that they happened. What occurred to her suddenly was an idea: 'Oh I'm such a crazy old bat.' Why, instead of continuing to ask about the people who weren't there, didn't she find the man and ask him how to get out of those passages? Because all she wanted was to get out and not run into anybody.

She finally found the man, while rounding a corner. And she spoke to him in a voice slightly tremulous and hoarse from exhaustion and fear of hoping in vain. The wary man agreed in a flash that the best thing for her to do really was go home and told her cautiously: 'Ma'am, you don't seem to be thinking straight, maybe it's this strange heat.'

Having said this, the man then simply accompanied her down the next passage and at the corner they spotted the two broad gates standing open. Simple as that? easy as that?

Simple as that.

Then the woman thought without coming to any conclusions that it was just for her that the exit had become impossible to find. Senhora Xavier was only slightly taken aback and at the same time used to it. Surely everyone had a path to follow interminably, this being part of destiny, though she didn't know whether she believed in that or not.

And there was the taxi passing. She hailed it and said to him controlling her voice that was becoming increasingly old and tired:

'Young man, I don't know the exact address, I've forgotten. But what I do know is that the house is on a street – I-don't-remember-which-anymore but something with "Gusmão" and the cross street if I'm not mistaken is Colonel-so-and-so.'

The driver was patient as with a child: 'All right now don't you get upset, let's calmly look for a street with "Gusmão" in the middle and "Colonel" at the end,' he said turning around with a smile and then winked at her with a conspiratorial look that seemed indecent. They took off with a jerk that rattled her insides.

Then suddenly she recognized the people she was looking for and who were to be found on the sidewalk in front of a big house. Yet it was as if the goal had been to get there and not to listen to the lecture that by then was completely forgotten, since Senhora Xavier had lost track of her objective. And she didn't know in the name of what she had walked so far. Then she realized she'd worn herself out beyond her own strength and wanted to leave, the lecture was a nightmare. So she asked a distinguished lady she was semi-acquainted with and who had a car with a driver to take her home because she wasn't feeling well in that strange heat. The chauffeur would only arrive in an hour. So Senhora Xavier sat in a chair they'd placed in the hallway for her, she sat bolt upright in her tight girdle, outside the culture being dissected across the way in the closed room. From which not a sound could be heard. She didn't really care about culture. And there she was in those labyrinths of 60 seconds and 60 minutes that would lead her to an hour.

Then the distinguished lady came and said: that there was a car for her out front but she was letting her know that, since her driver had said he was going to take a while, considering that you, ma'am, aren't feeling well, she had hailed the first taxi she saw. Why hadn't Senhora Xavier herself thought to call a taxi, instead of readily subjecting herself to the twists and turns of time spent waiting? Then Senhora Jorge B. Xavier thanked her with the utmost refinement. The woman had always been very refined and polite. She got into the taxi and said:

'Leblon, if you please.'

Her brain was hollow, it seemed like her head was fasting.

After a while she noticed they were driving around and around but that they kept ending up back at the same square. Why weren't they getting out of there? Was there

89

once again no way out? The driver ended up admitting that he wasn't familiar with the Zona Sul, that he only worked in the Zona Norte. And she didn't know how to give him directions. The cross of the years weighed ever more heavily on her and yet another lack of an exit merely revived the black magic of the passages of Maracanã. There was no way for them to be freed from the square! Then the driver told her to take another taxi, and he even flagged down one that was passing by. She thanked him stiffly, she was formal with people, even those she knew. Moreover she was very kind. In the new taxi she said fearfully:

'If it's not too much trouble, sir, let's go to Leblon.'

And they simply left the square at once and took different streets.

While unlocking the door to her apartment she had the urge, just in her head and fantasizing, to sob very loudly. But she wasn't the sort to sob or complain. In passing she told the maid she wouldn't be taking any phone calls. She went straight to her bedroom, took off all her clothes, swallowed a pill without water and then waited for it to take effect.

Meanwhile, she smoked. She remembered it was August and they say August brings bad luck. But September would arrive one day like an exit. And September was for some reason the month of May: a lighter and more transparent month. She vaguely pondered this until drowsiness finally set in and she fell asleep.

When she awoke hours later she saw then that a very fine, cool rain was coming down, it was cold as a knife blade. Naked in bed she was freezing. Then she thought that a naked old lady was a very curious thing. She remembered that she'd been planning to buy a wool scarf. She looked at the clock: the shops would still be open. She took a taxi and said:

'Ipanema, if you please.'

The man said:

'Sorry? Jardim Botânico?'

'Ipanema, please,' the woman repeated, quite surprised. It was the absurdity of total miscommunication: for, what did the words 'Ipanema' and 'Jardim Botânico' have in common? But once again she vaguely thought how 'her life was just like that.'

She quickly made her purchase and found herself on the already dark street with nothing to do. Because Senhor Jorge B. Xavier had traveled to São Paulo the day before and wouldn't be back until the next day.

Then, back home again, between taking another sleeping pill or doing something else, she opted for the second scenario, since she remembered she could now go back to looking for that misplaced bill of exchange. From what little she understood, that piece of paper represented money. Two days before she had exhaustively searched for it all over the house, even in the kitchen, but in vain. Now it occurred to her: and why not under the bed? Maybe. So she knelt on the floor. But she quickly got tired from putting all her weight on her knees and leaned on her two hands as well.

Then she realized she was on all fours.

She stayed that way awhile, perhaps meditative, perhaps not. Who knows, maybe Senhora Xavier was tired of being a human. She was being a bitch on all fours. Without the slightest nobility. Having shed her last bit of pride. On all fours, a little thoughtful perhaps. But all there was under the bed was dust.

She stood with concerted effort from her discombobulated joints and saw there was nothing else to do except realistically consider – and it was with a painstaking effort that she saw reality – realistically consider that the bill was lost for good and that keeping up the search would be never making it out of Maracanã.

And as always, since she'd given up the search, upon opening a little drawer of handkerchiefs to take one out – there was the bill of exchange.

Then the woman, tired from the effort of being on all fours, sat on the bed and completely out of nowhere started crying softly. It sounded more like some Arabic gibberish. She hadn't cried in 30 years, but now she was so tired. If crying was what that was. It wasn't. It was something. Finally she blew her nose. Then she had the following thought: that she would force the hand of 'destiny' and have a greater destiny. With willpower you can accomplish everything, she thought without the least conviction. And all this about being bound to a destiny had occurred to her because she had already started, without meaning to, thinking about 'that.'

But then it so happened that the woman also had the following thought: it was too late to have a destiny. She thought she would readily trade places with another being. That's when it occurred to her that there wasn't anyone to trade places with: no matter what she was, she was she and couldn't be transformed into another unique individual. Everyone was unique. So was Senhora Jorge B. Xavier.

But everything that had happened to her was still preferable to feeling 'that.' And that came with its long passages without an exit. 'That,' now with no shame at all, was the gnawing hunger in her guts, hunger to be possessed by that unattainable television idol. She never missed a single show of his. So, since she hadn't been able to keep from thinking about him, the thing to do was let herself think and recall the ladylike girl face of Roberto Carlos, my love.

She went to wash her dusty hands and caught sight of herself in the mirror above the sink. Then Senhora Xavier had this thought: 'If I really want it, really really want it, he'll be mine for at least one night.' She vaguely believed in willpower. Once again she had become entangled in a desire that was twisted and strangled.

But, who knows? If she gave up on Roberto Carlos, that's when things might happen between him and her. Senhora Xavier reflected a bit on the matter. Then she slyly pretended that she was giving up on Roberto Carlos. But she was well aware that the magic of giving up only produced positive results when it was real, and not just a ploy to get her way. Reality demanded a lot from the woman. She examined herself in the mirror to see if her face would become bestial under the influence of her feelings. But it was a subdued face that had long since stopped showing what she felt. Besides, her face had never expressed anything but good manners. And now it was merely the mask of a seventy-year-old woman. Then her lightly made-up face looked to her like a clown's. The woman faked a smile to see if that might improve things. It didn't.

From the outside – she saw in the mirror – she was a dried up thing like a dried fig. But on the inside she wasn't shriveled. Quite the contrary. On the inside she was like moist gums, soft just like toothless gums.

Then she searched for a thought that would make her spiritual or shrivel her once and for all. But she'd never been spiritual. And because of Roberto Carlos the woman was enveloped in the shadows of that matter in which she was profoundly anonymous.

Standing in the bathroom she was as anonymous as a chicken.

For a fraction of a fleeting second, she almost unconsciously glimpsed that all people are anonymous. Because no one is the other and the other didn't know the other. So – so the person is anonymous. And now she was tangled in that deep and fatal well, in the revolution of the body. A body whose depths were unseen and that was the darkness of the malignant shadows of her instincts, alive like lizards and rats. And everything out of season, fruit out of season? Why hadn't other old women warned her that this could happen up till the end? In old men she'd certainly witnessed leering glances. But not in old women. Out of season. And she, alive as if she were still somebody, she who wasn't anybody.

Senhora Jorge B. Xavier was nobody.

Then she wished for nice and romantic feelings in relation to the delicacy of Roberto Carlos's face. But she couldn't manage it: his delicacy merely led her to a dark passage of sensuality. And her damnation was lasciviousness. It was base hunger: she wanted to devour Roberto Carlos's mouth. She wasn't romantic, she was crude in matters of love. There in the bathroom, in front of the mirror above the sink.

With her indelibly sullied age.

Without at least a sublime thought that might serve as her rudder and ennoble her existence.

Then she began taking her hair out of its bun and combing it slowly. It needed to be colored again, its white roots were already showing. Then the woman had the following thought: in all my life there's never been a climax like in the stories you read. The climax was Roberto Carlos. She reflected, concluded that she would die secretly as she had secretly lived. But she also knew that every death is secret.

From the depths of her future death she thought she saw in the mirror the coveted figure of Roberto Carlos, with that soft wavy hair of his. There she was, trapped in desire out of season like that summer day in midwinter. Trapped in the tangle of passages in Maracanã. Trapped in the fatal secret of old women. It was just that she wasn't used to being nearly 70, she lacked practice and hadn't the slightest experience.

Then she said out loud and all alone:

'Robertinho Carlinhos.'

And to that she added: my love. She heard her voice in wonder as if making for the very first time, with no modesty or guilt whatsoever, the confession that all the same should have been shameful. The woman daydreamed that Robertinho might not want to accept her love because she herself was aware that this love was too sentimental, cloyingly voluptuous and greedy. And Roberto Carlos seemed so chaste, so asexual.

Were her lightly tinted lips still kissable? Or was it disgusting to kiss an old lady on the mouth? She studied her own lips up close and with no expression. And still with no expression she softly sang the chorus from Roberto Carlos's most famous song: 'I want you to keep me warm this winter and to hell with all the rest.'

That was when Senhora Jorge B. Xavier abruptly doubled over the sink as if about to vomit up her guts and interrupted her life with an earth-shattering silence: there! must! be! an! exiiiiiiit!

The Departure of the Train

The departure was from central station with its enormous clock, the biggest in the world. It showed six o'clock in the morning. Angela Pralini paid the taxi and took her small suitcase. Dona Maria Rita Alvarenga Chagas Souza Melo got out of her daughter's Opala and they headed toward the tracks. The old woman was dressed up and wearing jewelry. Emerging from the wrinkles that disguised her was the pure form of a nose lost in old age, and of a mouth that in times past must have been full and sensitive. But no matter. You reach a certain point – and it no longer matters what you were. A new race begins. An old woman cannot be communicated. She received the icy kiss from her daughter who left before the train departed. She used to help her board the train car. Since there was no center, she'd placed herself on the side. When the locomotive started moving, she was slightly taken aback: she hadn't expected the train to move in that direction and had sat facing backward.

Angela Pralini noticed her stirring and asked:

'Would you like to change places with me, ma'am?'

Dona Maria Rita gave a genteel start, said no, thank

you, she was fine where she was. But she seemed to have been shaken. She ran her hand over her gold filigree brooch, pinned to her breast, ran her hand over the clasp, took it off, raised it to her felt hat adorned with a fabric rose, took it off. Stern. Affronted? Finally she asked Angela Pralini:

'Is it on my account that you'd like to change places, miss?'

Angela Pralini said no, was surprised, the old woman surprised for the same reason: you don't accept favors from a little old lady. She smiled a bit too much and her powder-covered lips parted in dry furrows: she was charmed. And a bit worked up:

'How nice of you,' she said, 'how kind.'

There was a moment of disturbance because Angela Pralini laughed too, and the old woman kept laughing, revealing her well-polished dentures. She tugged discreetly at the girdle that was a little too tight.

'How nice,' she repeated.

She regained her composure somewhat quickly, crossed her hands over her purse that contained everything you could possibly imagine. Her wrinkles, as she'd been laughing, had taken on a meaning, thought Angela. Now they were once more incomprehensible, superimposed on a face that was once more unmalleable. But Angela had taken away her peace. She'd already seen lots of nervous girls telling themselves: if I laugh any more I'll ruin everything, it'll be ridiculous, I've got to stop – and it was impossible. The situation was very sad. With immense compassion, Angela saw the cruel wart on her chin, a wart with a sharp black hair poking out. But Angela had taken away her peace. You could tell she was about to smile any moment now: Angela had set the old woman on edge. Now she was one of those little old ladies who seem to think they're always late, that the appointed time has passed. A second later she couldn't contain herself, rose and peered out her window, as if it were impossible to stay seated.

'Do you want to open the window, ma'am?' said a young man listening to Handel on his transistor radio.

'Ah!' she exclaimed in terror.

Oh no! thought Angela, everything was getting ruined, the boy shouldn't have said that, it was too much, no one should have touched her again. Because the old woman, on the verge of losing the attitude which she lived off, on the verge of losing a certain bitterness, quivered like harpsichord music between smiling and being utterly charmed:

'No, no, no,' she said with false authority, 'not at all, thank you, I just wanted to look out.'

She sat immediately as if the young man and woman's consideration were keeping watch over her. The old woman, before boarding the train, had crossed her heart three times, discreetly kissing her fingertips. She was wearing a black dress with a real lace collar and a solid gold brooch. On her dark left hand were a widow's two thick wedding bands, thick like they don't make them anymore. From the next car a group of girl scouts could be heard singing a hymn to Brazil in high voices. Fortunately, in the next car. The music from the boy's radio mingled with another boy's music: he was listening to Edith Piaf who was singing 'J'attendrai.'

That had been when the train suddenly lurched and its wheels sprang into motion. The departure had begun. The old woman said softly: Oh Jesus! She bathed in the waters of Jesus. Amen. From a lady's transistor radio she learned it was six-thirty in the morning, a frigid morning. The old woman thought: Brazil was improving the signs along its highways. Someone named Kissinger seemed to be in charge of the world.

Nobody knows where I am, thought Angela Pralini, and that scared her a little, she was a fugitive.

'My name is Maria Rita Alvarenga Chagas Souza Melo – Alvarenga Chagas was my father's last name,' she added to beg pardon for having to utter so many words just to say her name. 'Chagas,' she added modestly, 'refers to the Wounds of Christ. But you can call me Dona Maria Ritinha. And your name? what's your Christian name?'

'My name is Angela Pralini. I'm going to spend six months on my aunt and uncle's farm. And you, ma'am?'

'Ah, I'm going to my son's farm, I'm going to spend the rest of my life there, my daughter brought me to the train and my son is waiting for me with the horse cart at the station. I'm like a package delivered from hand to hand.'

Angela's aunt and uncle didn't have children and treated her like a daughter. Angela recalled the note she'd left Eduardo: 'Don't try to find me. I'm going to disappear from you forever. I love you more than ever. Farewell. Your Angela stopped being yours because you didn't want her.'

They sat in silence. Angela Pralini let the rhythmic sounds of the train wash over her. Dona Maria Rita gazed once again at the diamond-and-pearl ring on her finger, adjusted her gold brooch: 'I'm old but I'm rich, richer than everyone in this car. I'm rich, I'm rich.' She peered at her watch, more to see its heavy gold case than to check the time. 'I'm very rich, I'm not just any old lady.' But she knew, ah she very well knew that she was just some little old lady, a little old lady frightened by the smallest things. She recalled herself, alone all day long in her rocking chair, alone with the servants, while her 'public relations' daughter spent all day out of the house, not coming home until eight at night, and without even giving her a kiss. She'd awoken that day at five in the morning, everything still dark, it was cold.

In the wake of the young man's consideration she was extraordinarily worked up and smiling. She seemed weakened. Her laugh revealed her to be one of those little old ladies full of teeth. The misplaced cruelty of teeth. The boy had already moved off. She opened and closed her eyelids. Suddenly she slapped her fingers against Angela's leg, extremely quickly and lightly:

'Today everyone is truly, just truly nice! so kind, so kind.'

Angela smiled. The old woman kept smiling without taking her deep, vacant eyes off the young woman's. Come on, come on they urged her all around, and she peered here and there as if to make a choice. Come on, come on! they pushed her laughing all around, and she shook with laughter, genteel.

'How nice everyone on this train is,' she said.

Suddenly she tried to regain her composure, pretended to clear her throat, got ahold of herself. It must have been hard. She feared she had reached a point of not being able to stop herself. She reined herself in severely and trembling, closed her lips over her innumerable teeth. But she couldn't fool anyone: her face held such hope that it disturbed any eyes that saw it. She no longer depended on anyone: once they had touched her, she could be on her way – she radiated on her own, thin, tall. She still would have liked to say anything at all and was already preparing some sociable head movement, full of studied charm. Angela wondered whether she'd manage to express herself. She seemed to think, think, and tenderly find a fully formed thought that might adequately couch her feelings. She said carefully and with the wisdom of the elders, as if she needed to act the part in order to speak like an old woman:

'Youth. Darling youth.'

Her laugh came out somewhat forced. Was she going

to have a nervous breakdown? thought Angela Pralini. Because she was so marvelous. But she cleared her throat again austerely, drummed her fingertips on the seat as if urgently summoning the orchestra to prepare a new score. She opened her purse, pulled out a little square of newspaper, unfolded it, unfolded it, until she turned it into a large, regular newspaper, dating from three days before – Angela saw from the date. She began to read.

Angela had lost over fifteen pounds. On the farm she'd gorge herself: black bean mash and collard greens, to gain back those precious lost pounds. She was so skinny from having gone along with Eduardo's brilliant and uninterrupted reasoning: she'd drink coffee without sugar nonstop in order to stay awake. Angela Pralini had very pretty breasts, they were her best feature. She had pointy ears and a pretty, curved mouth, kissable. Deep dark circles under her eyes. She made use of the train's screaming whistle as her own scream. It was a piercing howl, hers, only turned inward. She was the woman who drank the most whiskey in Eduardo's group. She could take 6 or 7 in a row, maintaining a terror-stricken lucidity. On the farm she'd drink creamy cow's milk. One thing united the old woman with Angela: both would be met with open arms, but neither knew this about the other. Angela suddenly shivered: who would give the dog its final dose of deworming treatment. Ah, Ulisses, she told the dog in her head, I didn't abandon you willingly, it's because I had to escape Eduardo, before he ruined me completely

103

with his lucidity: a lucidity that illuminated too much and singed everything. Angela knew that her aunt and uncle had antivenom for snake bites: she was planning to go straight into the heart of the dense and verdant forest, wearing tall boots and slathered in mosquito repellent. As if stepping off the Trans-Amazonian Highway, the explorer. What animals would she encounter? It was best to bring a rifle, food and water. And a compass. Ever since she'd discovered – but really discovered with a note of alarm – that she would die some day, then she no longer feared life, and, because of death, she had full rights: she'd risk everything. After having gone through two relationships that ended in nothing, this third was ending in love-adoration, cut off by the inevitability of the desire to survive. Eduardo had transformed her: he'd made her have eyes on the inside. But now she was looking outward. Through the window she saw the breasts of the land, in mountains. Little birds exist, Eduardo! clouds exist, Eduardo! a whole world of stallions and mares and cows exists, Eduardo, and when I was a little girl I would gallop on a bare horse, without a saddle! I'm fleeing my suicide, Eduardo. I'm sorry, Eduardo, but I don't want to die. I want to be fresh and rare like a pomegranate.

The old woman pretended to be reading the newspaper. But she was thinking: her world was a sigh. She didn't want others to think she'd been abandoned. God gave me health so I could travel alone. I'm also of sound mind, I don't talk to myself and I bathe by myself every day. She gave off the fragrance of wilted and crushed roses, it was her elderly, musty fragrance. To possess a breathing rhythm, Angela thought about the old woman, was the loveliest thing to have existed since Dona Maria Rita's birth. It was life.

Dona Maria Rita was thinking: once she got old she'd started to disappear to other people, they only glimpsed her. Old age: supreme moment. She was an outsider to the world's general strategy and her own was paltry. She'd lost track of her more far-reaching goals. She was already the future.

Angela thought: I think that if I happened upon the truth, I wouldn't be able to think it. It would be mentally unpronounceable.

The old woman had always been slightly empty, well, ever so slightly. Death? it was odd, it played no part in her days. And even 'not existing' didn't exist, not-existing was impossible. Not existing didn't fit into our daily life. Her daughter wasn't affectionate. In compensation her son was incredibly affectionate, good-natured, chubby. Her daughter was as brusque as her cursory kisses, the 'public relations' one. The old woman didn't feel quite up to living. The monotony, however, was what kept her going.

Eduardo would listen to music to accompany his thinking. And he *understood* the dissonance of modern music, all he knew how to do was *understand*. His intelligence that smothered her. You're a temperamental person,

Angela, he once told her. So what? What's wrong with that? I am what I am and not what you think I am. The proof that I am is in the departure of this train. My proof is also Dona Maria Rita, right there across from me. Proof of what? Yes. She'd already had plenitude. When she and Eduardo were so in love that while in the same bed, holding hands, they had felt life was complete. Few people have known plenitude. And, because plenitude is also an explosion, she and Eduardo had cowardly begun to live 'normally.' Because you can't prolong ecstasy without dying. They separated for a pointless, semi-invented reason: they didn't want to die of passion. Plenitude is one of those truths you happen upon. But the necessary split had been an amputation for her, just as there are women whose uterus and ovaries are removed. Empty inside.

Dona Maria Rita was so antique that people in her daughter's house were used to her like an old piece of furniture. She wasn't a novelty for anyone. But it had never crossed her mind that she was living in solitude. It was just that she didn't have anything to do. It was a forced leisure that at times became heartrending: she had nothing to do in the world. Except live like a cat, like a dog. Her ideal was to be a lady-in-waiting for some noble gentlewoman, but people didn't have them anymore and even so, no one would have believed in her hardy seventy-seven years, they'd have thought her feeble. She didn't do anything, all she did was this: be old. Sometimes she got depressed: she thought she was no good for anything, she was even no good for God. Dona Maria Ritinha didn't have hell inside her. Why did old people, even those who didn't tremble, evoke something delicately tremulous? Dona Maria Rita had a brittle tremor of accordion music.

But when it's a matter of life itself – who comes to our rescue? for each one stands alone. And each life must be rescued by that each-one's own life. Each one of us: that's what we count on. Since Dona Maria Rita had always been an average person, she thought dying wasn't a normal thing. Dying was surprising. It was as if she wasn't up to the act of death, for nothing extraordinary had ever happened to her in life up till now that could suddenly justify such an extraordinary fact. She talked and even thought about death, but deep down she was skeptical and suspicious. She thought you died when there was some disaster or someone killed someone else. The old woman had little experience. Sometimes she got palpitations: the heart's bacchanal. But that was it and even that dated back to girlhood. During her first kiss, for example, her heart had lost control. And it had been a good thing bordering on bad. Something that recalled her past, not as facts but as life: a sensation of shadowy vegetation, caladiums, giant ferns, maidenhair ferns, green freshness. Whenever she felt this all over again, she smiled. One of the most erudite words she used was 'picturesque.' It was good. It was like listening to the murmur of a spring and not knowing where it came from.

A dialogue she carried on with herself:

'Are you doing anything?'

'Yes I am: I am being sad.'

'Doesn't it bother you to be alone?'

'No, I think.'

Sometimes she didn't think. Sometimes a person sat there being. She didn't have to do. Being was already doing. You could be slowly or a bit fast.

In the row behind them, two women were talking and talking nonstop. Their constant sounds fused with the noise of the train wheels on the tracks.

As much as Dona Maria Rita had been hoping her daughter would wait on the train platform to give her a little sendoff, it didn't happen. The train motionless. Until it had lurched forward.

'Angela,' she said, 'a woman never tells her age, that's why all I can say is it's a lot of years. No, with you, Angela – can I use your first name? – with you I'm going to let you in on a secret: I'm seventy-seven years old.'

'I'm thirty-seven,' Angela Pralini said.

It was seven in the morning.

'When I was a girl I was such a little liar. I'd lie for no reason.'

Later, as if disenchanted with the magic of lying, she'd stopped.

Angela, looking at the elderly Dona Maria Rita, was afraid to grow old and die. Hold my hand, Eduardo, so I won't be afraid to die. But he didn't hold anything. All he did was: think, think and think. Ah, Eduardo, I want the sweetness of Schumann! Her life was a life undone, evanescent. She lacked a bone that was hard, tough and strong, that no one could cross. Who could be this essential bone? To distance herself from the sensation of overwhelming neediness, she thought: how did they get by in the Middle Ages without telephones or airplanes? Mystery. Middle Ages, I adore ye and thy black, laden clouds that opened onto the luminous and fresh Renaissance.

As for the old woman, she had checked out. She was gazing into the nothing.

Angela looked at herself in her compact. I look like I'm about to faint. Watch out for the abyss, I tell the woman who looks like she's about to faint. When I die I'll miss you so much, Eduardo! The declaration didn't stand up to logic yet possessed in itself an imponderable meaning. It was as if she wanted to express one thing and was expressing another.

The old woman was already the future. She seemed ashamed. Ashamed of being old? At some point in her life there certainly must have been a mistake, and the result was that strange state of life. Which nevertheless wasn't leading her to death. Death was always such a surprise for the person dying. Yet she took pride in not drooling or wetting the bed, as if that uncultivated form of health was the merited result of an act of her own will. The only reason she wasn't a grande dame, a distinguished older lady, was because she wasn't arrogant: she was a dignified little old lady who suddenly looked skittish. She – all right, she was praising herself, considered herself an old woman full of precociousness like a precocious child. But her life's true intention, she did not know.

Angela was dreaming about the farm: there you could hear shouts, barks and howls, at night. 'Eduardo,' she said to him in her head, 'I was tired of trying to be what you thought I am. There's a bad side – the stronger one and the one that dominated though I tried to hide it because of you – on that strong side I'm a cow, I'm a free horse that stamps at the ground, I'm a streetwalker, I'm a whore – and not a "woman of letters." I know I'm intelligent and that sometimes I hide it so I won't offend others with my intelligence, I who am a subconscious. I fled you, Eduardo, because you were killing me with that genius head of yours that made me nearly clap both hands over my ears and nearly scream with horror and exhaustion. And now I'm going to spend six months on the farm, you don't know where I'll be, and every day I'll bathe in the river mixing its mud with my own blessed clay. I'm common, Eduardo! and you should know that I like reading comics, my love, oh my love! how I love you and how I love your terrible incantations, ah how I adore you, slave of yours that I am. But I am physical, my love, I am physical and I had to hide from you the glory of being physical. And you, who are the very radiance of reasoning, though you don't know it, were nourished by me. You, super-intellectual and brilliant and leaving everyone stunned and speechless.'

'I think,' the old woman said to herself very slowly, 'I think that pretty girl isn't interested in chatting with me. I don't know why, but nobody chats with me anymore. And even when I'm with people, they don't seem to remember me. After all it's not my fault I'm old. But never mind, I keep myself company. And anyhow I've got Nandinho, my dear son who adores me.'

'The agonizing pleasure of scratching one's itch!' thought Angela. 'I, hmm, who never go in for this or that – I'm free!!! I'm getting healthier, oh I feel like blurting something really loud to scare everyone. Would the old woman get it? I don't know, she must have given birth plenty of times. I'm not falling into the trap of thinking the right thing to do is be unhappy, Eduardo. I want to enjoy everything and then die and be damned! be damned! be damned! Though the old woman might be unhappy without knowing it. Passivity. I won't go in for that either, no passivity whatsoever, what I want to do is bathe naked in the muddy river that resembles me, naked and free! hooray! Hip hip hooray! I'm abandoning everything! everything! and that way I won't be abandoned, I don't want to depend on more than around three people and for the rest it's: Hello, how are you? fine. Edu, you know what? I'm abandoning you. You, at the core of your intellectualism, aren't worth the life of a dog. I'm abandoning you, then. And I'm abandoning that group of pseudo-intellectuals that used to demand from me a vain and nervous constant exercise of false and hasty intelligence. I needed God to abandon me so I could feel his presence. I need to kill someone inside me. You ruined my intelligence with yours, a genius's. And forced me to know, to know, to know. Ah, Eduardo, don't worry, I've brought along the books you gave me so I can "follow a course of home study," as you wanted. I'll study philosophy by the river, out of the love I have for you.'

Angela Pralini had thoughts so deep there were no words to express them. It was a lie to say you could only have one thought at a time: she had many thoughts that intersected and were multiple. 'Not to mention the "subconscious" that explodes inside me, whether I want it to or you don't. I am a fount,' thought Angela, thinking at the same time about where she'd put her head scarf, thinking about whether the dog had drunk the milk she'd left him, Eduardo's shirts, and her extreme physical and mental depletion. And about elderly Dona Maria Rita. 'I'll never forget your face, Eduardo.' His was a somewhat astonished face, astonished at his own intelligence. He was naive. And he loved without knowing he was loving. He'd be beside himself when he found out that she'd left, leaving the dog and him. Abandonment due to lack of nutrition, she thought. At the same time she was thinking about the old woman sitting across from her. It wasn't true that you only think one thought at a time. She was, for example, capable of writing a check perfectly, without a single error, while thinking about her life, for example. Which wasn't good but in the end was hers. Hers again. Coherence, I don't want it anymore. Coherence is mutilation. I want disorder. I can only guess at it through a vehement incoherence. To meditate, I took myself out of me first and I feel the void. It is in the void that one passes the time. She who adored a nice day at the beach, with sun, sand and sun. Man is abandoned, has lost contact with the earth, with the sky. He no longer lives, he exists. The atmosphere between her and Eduardo Gosme was filled with emergency. He had transformed her into an urgent woman. And one who, to keep her urgency awake, took stimulants that made her thinner and thinner and took away her hunger. I want to eat, Eduardo, I'm hungry, Eduardo, hungry for lots of food! I am organic!

'Discover today the supertrain of tomorrow.' *Selections from the Reader's Digest* that she sometimes read in secret from Eduardo. It was like the *Selections* that said: discover today the supertrain of tomorrow. She positively wasn't discovering it today. But Eduardo was the supertrain. Super everything. She was discovering today the super of tomorrow. And she couldn't stand it. She couldn't stand the perpetual motion. You are the desert, and I am going to Oceania, to the South Seas, to the Isles of Tahiti. Though they're ruined by tourists. You're no more than a tourist, Eduardo. I'm headed for my own life, Edu. And I say like Fellini: in darkness and ignorance I create more.

The life I had with Eduardo smelled like a freshly painted new pharmacy. She preferred the living smell of manure disgusting as it was. He was correct like a tennis court. Incidentally, he played tennis to stay in shape. Anyway, he was a bore she used to love and almost no longer did. She was recovering her mental health right there on the train. She was still in love with Eduardo. And he, without knowing it, was still in love with her. I who can't get anything right, except omelets. With just one hand she'd crack eggs with incredible speed, and she cracked them into the bowl without spilling a single drop. Eduardo was consumed with envy at such elegance and efficiency. He sometimes gave lectures at universities and they adored him. She attended them too, she adoring him too. How was it again that he'd begin? 'I feel uncomfortable seeing people stand up when they hear I'm about to speak.' Angela was always afraid they'd walk out and leave him there alone.

The old woman, as if she'd received a mental transmission, was thinking: don't let them leave me alone. How old am I exactly? Oh I don't even know anymore.

Right afterward she let the thought drain away. And she was peacefully nothing. She hardly existed. It was good that way, very good indeed. Plunges into the nothing.

Angela Pralini, to calm down, told herself a very calming, very peaceful story: once upon a time there was a man who liked jabuticaba fruit very much. So he went to an orchard where there were trees laden with black, smooth and lustrous globules, that dropped into his hands in complete surrender and dropped from his hands to his feet. There was such an abundance of jabuticaba fruit that he gave in to the luxury of stepping on them. And they made a very delicious sound. They went like this: pop-pop-pop, etc. Angela grew calm like the jabuticaba man. There were jabuticabas on the farm and with her bare feet she'd make that soft, moist 'pop-pop.' She never knew whether or not you were supposed to swallow the pits. Who would answer that question? No one. Perhaps only a man who, like Ulisses, the dog, and unlike Eduardo, would answer: '*Mangia, bella, que te fa bene.*'* She knew a little Italian but was never sure whether she had it right. And, after what that man said, she'd swallow the pits. Another delicious tree was one whose scientific name she had forgotten but that in childhood everyone had known directly, without science, it was one that in the Rio Botanical Garden made a dry little 'pop-pop.' See? see how you're being reborn? The cat's seven breaths. The number seven followed her everywhere, it was her secret, her strength. She felt beautiful. She wasn't. But that's how she felt. She also felt kindhearted. With tenderness toward the elderly Maria Ritinha who had put on her glasses and was reading the newspaper. Everything about the elderly Maria Rita was meandering. Near the end? oh, how it hurts to die. In life you suffer but you're

* Italian: 'Eat, pretty girl, it's good for you.'

holding on to something: ineffable life. And as for the question of death? You mustn't be afraid: go forward, always.

Always.

Like the train.

Somewhere there's something written on the wall. And it's for me, thought Angela. From the flames of Hell a fresh telegram will arrive for me. And never again will my hope be disappointed. Never. Never again.

The old woman was anonymous as a chicken, as some-one named Clarice had said talking about a shameless old woman, in love with Roberto Carlos. That Clarice made people uncomfortable. She made the old woman shout: there! must! be! an! exiiit! And there was. For example, the exit for that old woman was the husband who'd be home the next day, it was the people she knew, it was her maid, it was the intense and fruitful prayer in the face of despair. Angela told herself as if furiously bit-ing herself: there must be an exit. As much for me as for Dona Maria Rita.

I couldn't stop time, thought Maria Rita Alvarenga Cha-gas Souza Melo. I've failed. I'm old. And she pretended to read the newspaper just to gain some composure.

I want shade, Angela moaned, I want shade and anonymity.

The old woman thought: her son was so kindhearted, so warm, so affectionate! He called her 'dear little mother.' Yes, maybe I'll spend the rest of my life on the farm, far from 'public relations' who doesn't need me. And my life should be very long, judging by my parents and grand-parents. I could easily, easily, make it to a hundred, she thought comfortably. And die suddenly so I won't have time to be afraid. She crossed herself discreetly and prayed to God for a good death.

Ulisses, if his face were viewed from a human perspec-tive, would be monstrous and ugly. He was beautiful from a dog's perspective. He was vigorous like a white and free horse, only he was a soft brown, orangish, whiskey-colored. But his coat is beautiful like that of an energetic rearing horse. The muscles of his neck were vigorous and people could grasp those muscles in hands with knowing fingers. Ulisses was a man. Without the dog-eat-dog world. He was refined like a man. A woman should treat her man well.

The train entering the countryside: the crickets were calling, shrill and hoarse.

Eduardo, every once in a while, awkwardly like some-one forced to fulfill a duty – gave her an ice-cold diamond as a present. She who was partial to sparkling gems. Any-how, she sighed, things are the way they are. At times she felt, whenever she looked down from high in her apart-ment, the urge to commit suicide. Ah, not because of Eduardo but from a kind of fatal curiosity. She didn't tell anyone this, afraid of influencing a latent suicide. She wanted life, a level and full life, very laid-back, very much reading *Reader's Digest* in the open. She didn't want to die until she was ninety, in the midst of some act of life, without feeling anything. What are you doing? I'm waiting for the future.

When the train had finally started moving, Angela Pralini lit a cigarette in hallelujah: she'd been worried that, until the train departed, she wouldn't have the courage to go and would end up leaving the car. But right after, they were subjected to the deafening yet sudden jerking of the wheels. The train was chugging along. And old Maria Rita was sighing: she was that much closer to her beloved son. With him she could be a mother, she who was castrated by her daughter.

Once when Angela was suffering from menstrual cramps, Eduardo had tried, rather awkwardly, to be affectionate. And he'd said something horrifying to her: you have an ouchy, don't you? It was enough to make her flush with embarrassment.

The train sped along as fast as it could. The happy engineer: that's how I like it, and he blew the whistle at every curve in the rails. It was the long, hearty whistle of a moving train, making headway. The morning was cool and full of tall green grasses. That's it, yes sir, come on, said the engineer to the engine. The engine responded with joy.

The old woman was nothing. And she was looking at the air as one looks at God. She was made of God. That is: all or nothing. The old woman, thought Angela, was vulnerable. Vulnerable to love, love for her son. The mother was Franciscan, the daughter was pollution.

God, Angela thought, if you exist, show yourself! Because it was time. It's this hour, this minute and this second.

And the result was that she had to hide the tears that sprang to her eyes. God had her. She was satisfied and stifled a muffled sob. How living hurt. Living was an open wound. Living is being like my dog. Ulisses has nothing to do with Joyce's Ulysses. I tried to read Joyce but stopped because he was boring, sorry, Eduardo. Still, a brilliant bore. Angela was loving the old woman who was nothing, the mother she lacked. A sweet, naive, long-suffering mother. Her mother who had died when she turned nine. Even sick but alive was good enough. Even paralyzed.

The air between Eduardo and her tasted like Saturday. And suddenly the two of them were rare, rarity in the air. They felt rare, not part of the thousand people wandering the streets. The two of them were sometimes conspiratorial, they had a secret life because no one would understand them. And also because the rare ones are persecuted by the people who don't tolerate the insulting offense of those who are different. They hid their love so as not to wound the eyes of others with envy. So as not to wound them with a spark too luminous for the eyes.

Bow, wow, wow, my dog had barked. My big dog.

The old woman thought: I'm an involuntary person. So much that, when she laughed – which was rare – you couldn't tell whether she was laughing or crying. Yes. She was involuntary.

Meanwhile there was Angela Pralini effervescing like the bubbles in Caxambu mineral water, she was one: all of a sudden. Just like that: suddenly. Suddenly what? Just suddenly. Zero. Nothing. She was thirty-seven and planning at any moment to start her life over. Like the little effervescent bubbles in Caxambu water. The seven letters in Pralini gave her strength. The seven letters in Angela made her anonymous.

With a long, howling whistle, they arrived at the little station where Angela Pralini would get off. She took her suitcase. In the space between a porter's cap and a young woman's nose, there was the old woman sleeping stiffly, her head erect beneath her felt hat, a fist closed on the newspaper.

Angela left the train.

Naturally this hadn't the slightest importance: there are people who are always led to regret, it's a trait of certain guilty natures. But what kept disturbing her was the vision of the old woman when she awoke, the image of her astonished face across from Angela's empty seat. After all who knew if she had fallen asleep out of trust in her.

Trust in the world.

Report on the Thing

This thing is the most difficult for a person to understand. Keep trying. Don't get discouraged. It will seem obvious. But it is extremely difficult to know about it. For it involves time.

We divide time when in reality it is not divisible. It is always immutable. But we need to divide it. And to that end a monstrous thing was created: the clock.

I am not going to speak of clocks. But of one particular clock. I'm showing my cards: I'll say up front what I have to say and without literature. This report is the anti-literature of the thing.

The clock of which I speak is electronic and has an alarm. The brand is Sveglia, which means 'wake up.' Wake up to what, my God? To time. To the hour. To the instant. This clock is not mine. But I took possession of its infernal tranquil soul.

It is not a wristwatch: therefore it is freestanding. It is less than an inch tall and stands on the surface of the table. I would like its actual name to be Sveglia. But the clock's owner wants its name to be Horácio. No matter. Because the main thing is that it is time.

Its mechanism is very simple. It does not have the complexity of a person but it is more people than people. Is it a superman? No, it comes straight from the planet Mars, so it seems. If that's where it is from then that's where it will one day return. It is silly to state that it does not need to be wound, since this is the case with other timepieces, as with mine that's a wristwatch, that's shock resistant, that can get wet as you like. Those are even more than people. But at least they are from Earth. The Sveglia is from God. Divine human brains were used to capture what this watch should be. I am writing about it but have yet to see it. It will be the Encounter. Sveglia: wake up, woman, wake up to see what must be seen. It is important to be awake in order to see. But it is also important to sleep in order to dream about the lack of time. Sveglia is the Object, it is the Thing, with a capital letter. I wonder, does the Sveglia see me? Yes, it does, as if I were another object. It recognizes that sometimes we too come from Mars.

Things have been happening to me, after I found out about the Sveglia, that seem like a dream. Wake me up, Sveglia, I want to see reality. But then, reality resembles a dream. I am melancholy because I am happy. It is not a paradox. After the act of love don't you feel a certain melancholy? That of plenitude. I feel like crying. Sveglia does not cry. Besides, it has no way to. Does its energy have any weight? Sleep, Sveglia, sleep a little, I can't stand your constant vigil. You never stop being. You never dream. It cannot be said that you 'function': you are not the act of functioning, you just are.

You are just so thin. And nothing happens to you. But you are the one who makes things happen. Happen to me, Sveglia, happen to me. I am in need of a certain event of which I cannot speak. And bring back desire to me, which is the coil spring behind animal life. I do not want you for myself. I do not like being watched. And you are the only eye always open like an eye floating in space. You wish me no harm but neither do you wish me good. Could I be getting that way too, without the feeling of love? Am I a thing? I know that I have little capacity to love. My capacity to love has been trampled too much, my God. All I have left is a flicker of desire. I *need* this to be strengthened. Because it is not as you think, that only death matters. To live, something you don't know about because it is susceptible to rot – to live while rotting matters quite a bit. A harsh way to live: a way to live the essential.

If it breaks, do they think it died? No, it simply departed itself. But you have weaknesses, Sveglia. I learned from your owner that you need a leather case to protect you from humidity. I also learned, in secret, that you once stopped. Your owner didn't panic. She fiddled with it a little and you never stopped again. I understand you, I forgive you: you came from Europe and you need a little time to get acclimated, don't you? Does that mean that you die too, Sveglia? Are you the time that stops?

I once heard, over the phone, the Sveglia's alarm go off. It is like inside us: we wake up from the inside out. It seems its electronic-God communicates with our electronic-God brain: the sound is low, not the least bit shrill. Sveglia ambles like a white horse roaming free and saddleless.

I learned of a man who owned a Sveglia and to whom Sveglia happened. He was walking with his ten-year-old son, at night, and the son said: watch out, Father, there's voodoo out there. The father recoiled – but wouldn't you know he stepped right on a burning candle, snuffing it out? Nothing seemed to have happened, which is also very Sveglia. The man went to bed. When he awoke he saw that one of his feet was swollen and black. He called some doctor friends who saw no sign of injury: the foot was intact – only black and very swollen, the kind of swelling that stretches the skin completely taut. The doctors called more colleagues. And nine doctors decided it was gangrene. They had to amputate the foot. They made an appointment for the next day and an exact time. The man fell asleep.

And he had a terrible dream. A white horse was trying to attack him and he was fleeing like a madman. This all took place in the Campo de Santana. The white horse was beautiful and adorned with silver. But there was no escape. The horse got him right on the foot, trampling it. That's when the man awoke screaming. They thought it was nerves, explained that these things happened right before an operation, gave him a sedative, he went back to sleep. When he awoke, he immediately looked at his foot. Surprise: the foot was white and its normal size. The nine doctors came and couldn't explain it. They didn't know about the enigma of the Sveglia against which only a white horse can fight. There was no longer any reason to operate. Only, he can't put any weight on that foot: it was weakened. It was the sign of the horse harnessed with silver, of the snuffed candle, of the Sveglia. But Sveglia wanted to be victorious and something happened. That man's wife, in perfect health, at the dinner table, started feeling sharp pains in her intestines. She cut dinner short and went to lie down. The husband, worried sick, went to check on her. She was white, drained of blood. He took her pulse: there was none. The only sign of life was that her forehead was pearled with sweat. He called the doctor who said it might be a case of catalepsy. The husband didn't agree. He uncovered her stomach and made simple movements over her – the same he himself made when Sveglia had stopped – movements he couldn't explain.

The wife opened her eyes. She was in perfect health. And she's alive, may God keep her.

This has to do with Sveglia. I don't know how. But that it does, no question. And what about the white horse of the Campo de Santana, which is a plaza full of little birds, pigeons and coatis? In full regalia, trimmed in silver, with a lofty and bristling mane. Running rhythmically in counterpoint to Sveglia's rhythm. Running without haste.

I am in perfect physical and mental health. But one night I was sleeping soundly and could be heard saying in a loud voice: I want to have a baby with Sveglia!

I believe in the Sveglia. It doesn't believe in me. It thinks I lie a lot. And I do. On Earth we lie a lot.

I went five years without catching the flu: that is Sveglia. And when I did it lasted three days. Afterward a dry cough lingered. But the doctor prescribed antibiotics and I got better. Antibiotics are Sveglia.

This is a report. Sveglia does not allow short stories or novels no matter what. It only permits transmission. It hardly allows me to call this a report. I call it a report on the mystery. And I do my best to write a report dry as extra-dry champagne. But sometimes – forgive me – it gets wet. A dry thing is sterling silver. Whereas gold is wet. May I speak of diamonds in relation to Sveglia?

No, it just is. And in fact Sveglia has no intimate name: it preserves its anonymity. Besides, God has no name: he preserves perfect anonymity: there is no language that utters his true name.

Sveglia is dumb: it acts covertly without premeditation. I am now going to say a very serious thing that will seem like heresy: God is dumb. Because he does not understand, he does not think, he just is. It is true that it's a kind of dumbness that executes itself. But He commits many errors. And knows it. Just look at us who are a grave error. Just look how we organize ourselves into society and intrinsically, from one to another. But there is one error He does not commit: He does not die.

Sveglia does not die either. I have still not seen the Sveglia, as I have mentioned. Perhaps seeing it is wet. I know everything about it. But its owner does not want me to see it. She is jealous. Jealousy eventually drips from being so wet. Anyhow, our Earth risks becoming wet with feelings. The rooster is Sveglia. The egg is pure Sveglia. But the egg only when whole, complete, white, its shell dry, completely oval. Inside it is life; wet life. But eating raw yolk is Sveglia.

Do you want to see who Sveglia is? A football match. Whereas Pelé is not. Why? Impossible to explain. Perhaps he didn't respect anonymity.

Fights are Sveglia. I just had one with the clock's owner. I said: since you don't want to let me see Sveglia, describe its gears to me. Then she lost her temper – and that is Sveglia – and said she had a lot of problems – having problems is not Sveglia. So I tried to calm her down and it was fine. I won't call her tomorrow. I'll let her rest.

It seems to me that I will write about the electronic thing without ever seeing it. It seems it will have to be that way. It is fated.

I am sleepy. Could that be permitted? I know that dreaming is not Sveglia. Numbers are permitted. Though six is not. Very few poems are permitted. Novels, then, forget it. I had a maid for seven days, named Severina, who had gone hungry as a child. I asked if she was sad. She said she was neither happy nor sad: she was just that way. She was Sveglia. But I was not and couldn't stand the absence of feeling.

Sweden is Sveglia.

But now I am going to sleep though I shouldn't dream.

Water, despite being wet *par excellence*, is. Writing is. But style is not. Having breasts is. The male organ is too much. Kindness is not. But not-kindness, giving oneself, is. Kindness is not the opposite of meanness.

Will my writing be wet? I think so. My last name is. Whereas my first name is too sweet, it is meant for love. Not having any secrets – and yet maintaining the enigma – is Sveglia. In terms of punctuation ellipses are not. If someone understands this undisclosed and precise report of mine, that someone is. It seems that I am not I, because I am so much I. The Sun is, not the Moon. My face is. Probably yours is too. Whiskey is. And, as incredible as it might seem, Coca-Cola is, while Pepsi never was. Am I giving free advertising? That's wrong, you hear, Coca-Cola?

Being faithful is. The act of love contains in itself a desperation that is.

Now I am going to tell a story. But first I would like to say that the person who told me this story was someone who, despite being incredibly kind, is Sveglia.

Now I am nearly dying of exhaustion. Sveglia – if we aren't careful – kills.

The story goes like this:

It takes place in a locale called Coelho Neto, in the State of Guanabara. The woman in the story was very unhappy because her leg was wounded and the wound wouldn't heal. She worked very hard and her husband was a postman. Being a postman is Sveglia. They had many children. Almost nothing to eat. But that postman had been instilled with the responsibility of making his wife happy. Being happy is Sveglia. And the postman resolved to resolve the situation. He pointed out a neighbor who was barren and suffered greatly from this. She just couldn't get pregnant. He pointed out to his wife how happy she was because she had children. And she became happy, even with so little food. The postman also pointed out how another neighbor had children but her husband drank a lot and beat her and the children. Whereas he didn't drink and had never hit his wife or the children. Which made her happy.

Every night they felt sorry for their barren neighbor and for the one whose husband beat her. Every night they were very happy. And being happy is Sveglia. Every night.

I was hoping to reach page 9 on the typewriter. The number nine is nearly unattainable. The number 13 is God. The typewriter is. The danger of its no longer being Sveglia comes when it gets a little mixed up with the feelings of the person who's writing.

I got sick of Consul cigarettes which are menthol and sweet. Whereas Carlton cigarettes are dry, they're rough, they're harsh, and do not cooperate with the smoker. Since everything is or isn't, it doesn't bother me to give free advertising for Carlton. But, as for Coca-Cola, I don't excuse it.

I want to send this report to *Senhor* magazine and I want them to pay me very well.

Since you are, why don't you judge whether my cook, who cooks well and sings all day, is.

I think I'll conclude this report that is essential for explaining the energetic phenomena of matter. But I don't know what to do. Ah, I'll go get dressed.

See you never, Sveglia. The deep blue sky is. The waves white with sea foam are, more than the sea. (I have already bid farewell to Sveglia, but will keep speaking about it strictly because I can't help it, bear with me). The smell of the sea combines male and female and in the air a son is born that is.

The clock's owner told me today that it's the one that owns her. She told me that it has some tiny black holes from which a low sound comes out like an absence of words, the sound of satin. It has an internal gear that is golden. The external gear is silver, nearly colorless – like an aircraft in space, flying metal. Waiting, is it or isn't it? I don't know how to answer because I suffer from urgency and am rendered incapable of judging this item without getting emotionally involved. I don't like waiting.

A musical quartet is immensely more so than a symphony. The flute is. The harpsichord has an element of terror in it: the sounds come out rustling and brittle. Something from an otherworldly soul.

Sveglia, when will you finally leave me in peace? You aren't going to stalk me for the rest of my life transforming it into the brightness of everlasting insomnia, are you? Now I hate you. Now I would like to be able to write a story: a short story or a novel or a transmission. What will be my future step in literature? I suspect I won't write anymore. But it's true that at other times I have suspected this yet still wrote. What, however, must I write, my God? Was I contaminated by the mathematics of Sveglia and will I only be able to write reports?

And now I am going to end this report on the mystery. It so happens that I am very tired. I'll take a shower before going out and put on a perfume that is my secret. I'll say just one thing about it: it is rustic and a bit harsh, with hidden sweetness. It is.

Farewell, Sveglia. Farewell forever never. You already killed a part of me. I died and am rotting. Dying is.

And now – now farewell.

The Sound of Footsteps

She was eighty-one years old. Her name was Mrs Cândida Raposo.

Life made this old woman dizzy. The dizziness got worse whenever she spent a few days on a farm: the altitude, the green of the trees, the rain, they all made it worse. Whenever she listened to Liszt she got goosebumps all over. She'd been a beauty in her youth. And she got dizzy whenever she deeply inhaled the scent of a rose.

It so happened that for Mrs Cândida Raposo the desire for pleasure didn't go away.

She finally mustered the great courage to see a gynecologist. And she asked him, ashamed, eyes downcast:

'When will it go away?'

'When will what go away, ma'am?'

'The thing.'

'What thing?'

'The thing,' she repeated. 'The desire for pleasure,' she finally said.

'Ma'am, I'm sorry to say it never goes away.'

She stared at him in shock.

'But I'm eighty-one years old!'

'It doesn't matter, ma'am. It lasts until we die.'

'But that's hell!'

'That's life, Mrs Raposo.'

So that was life, then? this shamelessness?

'So what am I supposed to do? no one wants me anymore . . .'

The doctor looked at her with compassion.

'There's no cure for it, ma'am.'

'And what if I paid?'

'It wouldn't matter. You've got to remember, ma'am, you're eighty-one years old.'

'And . . . and what if I took care of it myself? do you know what I mean?'

'Yes,' said the doctor. 'That might be a remedy.'

Then she left the doctor's office. Her daughter was waiting down below, in the car. Cândida Raposo had lost a son in World War II, he was a soldier. She had this unbearable pain in her heart: that of surviving someone she loved.

That same night she found a way to satisfy herself on her own. Mute fireworks.

Afterward she cried. She was ashamed. From then on she'd use the same method. Always sad. That's life, Mrs Raposo, that's life. Until the blessing of death.

Death.

She thought she heard the sound of footsteps. The footsteps of her husband Antenor Raposo.

Brasília

Brasília is constructed on the line of the horizon. Brasília is artificial. As artificial as the world must have been when it was created. When the world was created, a man had to be created especially for that world. We are all deformed by our adaptation to the freedom of God. We don't know how we would be if we had been created first and the world were deformed after according to our requirements. Brasília does not yet have the Brasília man. If I said that Brasília is pretty they would immediately see that I liked the city. But if I say that Brasília is the image of my insomnia they would see this as an accusation. But my insomnia is neither pretty nor ugly, my insomnia is me myself, it is lived, it is my astonishment. It is a semicolon. The two architects didn't think of building beauty, that would be easy: they erected inexplicable astonishment. Creation is not a comprehension, it is a new mystery. – When I died, one day I opened my eyes and there was Brasília. I was alone in the world. There was a parked taxi. Without a driver. Oh how frightening. – Lúcio Costa and Oscar Niemeyer, two solitary men. – I regard Brasília as I regard Rome:

Brasília began with a final simplification of ruins. The ivy has yet to grow.

Besides the wind there is something else that blows. One can only recognize it by the supernatural rippling of the lake. – Wherever people stand, children might fall, and off the face of the world. Brasília lies at the edge. – If I lived here I would let my hair grow to the ground. – Brasília has a splendored past that now no longer exists. This type of civilization disappeared millennia ago. In the 4th century BC it was inhabited by extremely tall blond men and women who were neither Americans nor Swedes and who sparkled in the sun. They were all blind. That is why in Brasília there is nothing to stumble into. The Brasilianaires dressed in white gold. The race went extinct because few children were born. The more beautiful the Brasilianaires were, the blinder and purer and more sparkling, and the fewer children. The Brasilianaires lived for nearly three hundred years. There was nothing in the name of which to die. Millennia later it was discovered by a band of outcasts who would not have been welcomed anywhere else: they had nothing to lose. There they lit fires, pitched tents, gradually digging away at the sands that buried the city. These were men and women, smaller and dark, with darting and uneasy eyes, and who, being fugitives and desperate, had something in the name of which to live and die. They dwelled in ruined houses, multiplied, establishing a deeply contemplative race of humans. – I waited for nightfall like someone waiting for the shadows so as to steal out. When night fell I realized in horror that it was no use: no matter where I was I would be seen. What terrifies me is: seen by whom? – It was built with no place for rats. A whole part of us, the worst, precisely the one horrified by rats, that part has no place in Brasília. They wished to deny that we are worthless. A construction with space factored in for the clouds. Hell understands me better. But the rats, all huge, are invading. That is an invisible headline in the newspapers. – Here I am afraid. – The construction of Brasília: that of a totalitarian State. – This great visual silence that I love. My insomnia too would have created this peace of the never. I too, like those two who are monks, would meditate in this desert. Where there's no place for temptation. But I see in the distance vultures hovering. What could be dying, my God? – I didn't cry once in Brasília. There was no place for it. – It is a beach without the sea. – In Brasília there is no way in, and no way out. – Mama, it's lovely to see you standing there in that fluttering white cape. (It's because I died, my son). – An open-air prison. In any case there would be nowhere to escape. Because whoever escapes would probably go to Brasília. – They imprisoned me in freedom. But freedom is only what can be conquered. When they grant it to me, they are ordering me to be free. – A whole side of human coldness that I possess, I encounter in myself here in Brasília, and it blossoms ice-cold, potent, ice-cold force of Nature. This is the place where my crimes (not the worst, but those I won't ever understand in myself), where my ice-cold crimes find space. I am leaving. Here my crimes would not be those of love. I am leaving on behalf of my other crimes, those that God and I comprehend. But I know I shall return. I am drawn here by whatever frightens me in myself. – I have never seen anything like it in the world. But I recognize this city in the furthest depths of my dream. The furthest depths of my dream is a lucidity. – Well as I was saying, Flash Gordon . . . – If they took my picture standing in Brasília, when they developed the photograph only the landscape would appear. – Where are Brasília's giraffes? – A certain cringing of mine, certain silences, make my son say: gosh, grown-ups are the worst. – It's urgent. If it doesn't get populated, or rather, overpopulated, it will be too late: there will be no place for people. They will feel tacitly expelled. – The soul here casts no shadow on the ground. – For the first couple of days I wasn't hungry. Everything looked to me like airplane food. – At night I reached my face toward the silence. I know there is a hidden hour when manna descends and moistens the lands of Brasília. – No matter how close one gets, everything here is seen from afar. I couldn't find a way to touch. But at least I had this in my favor: before I got here, I already knew how to touch from afar. I never got too discouraged: from afar, I would touch. I've had a lot, and not even what I touched, you know. That's how rich women are. Pure Brasília. – The city of Brasília lies beyond the city. – *Boys, boys, come here, will you, look who is coming on the street all dressed up in modernistic style. It ain't nobody but . . . (Aunt Hagar's Blues, Ted Lewis and His Band, with Jimmy Dorsey on the clarinet.)* – That frightening beauty, this city, drawn up in the air. – For now no samba can spring up in Brasília. – Brasília doesn't let me get tired. It pursues a little. Feeling good, feeling good, feeling good, I'm in a good mood. And after all I have always cultivated my weariness, as my richest passivity. – All this is just today. Only God knows what will happen in Brasília. Because here chance is abrupt. – Brasília is haunted. It is the still profile of a thing. – In my insomnia I look out the hotel window at three in the morning. Brasília is the landscape of insomnia. It never falls asleep. – Here the organic being does not decompose. It is petrified. – I would like to see scattered through Brasília five hundred thousand eagles of the blackest onyx. – Brasília is asexual. – The First instant of seeing is like a certain instant of drunkenness: your feet don't touch the ground. – How deeply we breathe in Brasília. Whoever breathes starts to desire. And to desire is what one cannot do. There isn't any. Will there ever be? The thing is, I am not seeing where. – I wouldn't be shocked to run into Arabs in the street. Arabs, ancient and dead. – Here my passion dies. And I gain a lucidity that leaves me grandiose for no reason. I am fabulous and useless, I am made of pure gold. And almost psychic. – If there is any crime humanity has yet to commit, that new crime will be inaugurated here.

And so hardly kept secret, so well-suited to the high plain, that no one would ever know. – Here is the place where space most resembles time. – I am sure this is my rightful place. But the thing is, I am too addicted to the land. I have bad life habits. – Erosion will strip Brasília to the bone. – The religious atmosphere I felt from the first instant, and that I denied. This city has been achieved through prayer. Two men beatified by solitude created me standing here, restless, alone, out in this wind. – Brasília badly needs roaming white horses. At night they would be green in the moonlight. – I know what the two wanted: slowness and silence, which is also my idea of eternity. The two created the picture of an eternal city. – There is something here that frightens me. When I figure out what it is that frightens me, I shall also know what I love here. Fear has always guided me toward what I desire. And because I desire, I fear. Often it was fear that took me by the hand and led me. Fear leads me to danger. And everything I love is risky. – In Brasília are the craters of the Moon. – The beauty of Brasília is its invisible statues.

I went to Brasília in 1962. What I wrote about it is what you have just read. And now I have returned twelve years later for two days. And I wrote about it too. So here is everything I vomited up.

Warning: I am about to begin.

This piece is accompanied by Strauss's 'Vienna Blood' waltz. It's 11:20 on the morning of the 13th.

BRASÍLIA: SPLENDOR

Brasília is an abstract city. And there is no way to make it concrete. It is a rounded city with no corners. Neither does it have any neighborhood bars for people to get a cup of coffee. It's true, I swear I didn't see any corners. In Brasília the everyday does not exist. The cathedral begs God. It is two hands held open to receive. But Niemeyer is an ironic man: he has ironized life. It is sacred. Brasília does not allow the diminutive. Brasília is a joke, strictly perfect and without error. And the only thing that saves me is error.

The São Bosco church has such splendid stained glass that I fell silent seated on the pew, not believing it was real. Moreover the age we are passing through is fantastical, it is blue and yellow, and scarlet and emerald. My God, but what wealth. The stained glass holds light made of organ music. This church thus illuminated is nevertheless inviting. The only flaw is the unusual circular chandelier that looks like some nouveau riche thing. The church would have been pure without the chandelier. But what can you do? go at night, in the dark, and steal it?

Then I went to the National Library. A young Russian girl named Kira helped me. I saw young men and women studying and flirting: something totally compatible. And praiseworthy, of course.

I pause for a moment to say that Brasília is a tennis court.

There is a reinvigorating chill there. What hunger, but what hunger. I asked if the city had a lot of crime. I was told that in the suburb of Grama (is that its name?) there are about three homicides per week. (I interrupted the crimes to eat.) The light of Brasília left me blind. I forgot my sunglasses at the hotel and was invaded by a terrible white light. But Brasília is red. And is completely naked. There is no way for people not to be exposed in that city. Although the air is unpolluted: you can breathe well, a little too well, your nose gets dry.

Naked Brasília leaves me beatified. And crazy. In Brasília I have to think in parentheses. Will they arrest me for living? That's exactly it.

I am no more than phrases overheard by chance. On the street, while crossing through traffic, I heard: 'It was out of necessity.' And at the Roxy Cinema, in Rio de Janeiro, I heard two fat women saying: 'In the morning she slept and at night she woke up.' 'She has no stamina.' In Brasília I have stamina, whereas in Rio I am sort of languid, sort of sweet. And I heard the following phrase from the same fat women who were short: 'Just what does she have to go do over there?' And that, my dears, is how I got expelled.

Brasília has euphoria in the air. I said to the driver of the yellow cab: today seems like Monday, doesn't it? 'Yep,' he answered. And nothing more was said. I wanted so badly to tell him I had been to the utterly adored Brasília. But he didn't want to hear it. Sometimes I'm too much.

Then I went to the dentist, got that, Brasília? I take care of myself. Should I read odontology journals just because I'm in the dentist's waiting room? After I sat in the dentist's magnificent death chair, electric chair, and saw a machine looking at me, called 'Atlas 200.' It looked in vain, since I had no cavities. Brasília has no cavities. A powerful land, that one. And it doesn't mess around. It bets high and plays to win. Merquior and I burst into howls of laughter that are still echoing back to me in Rio. I have been irremediably impregnated by Brasília.

I prefer the Carioca entanglement. I was delicately pampered in Brasília but scared to death of reading my lecture. (Here I note an event that astonishes me: I am writing in the past, present and future. Am I being levitated? Brasília suffers from levitation.) I throw myself into each one, I'm telling you. But it is good because it is risky. Believe it or not: as I was reading the words, I was praying inwardly. But, again, it is good because it is risky. Now I wonder: if there are no corners, where do the prostitutes stand smoking? do they sit on the ground? And the beggars? do they have cars? because there you can only get around by car.

The light in Brasília sometimes leads to ecstasy and total plenitude. But it is also aggressive and harsh – ah, how I would like the shade of a tree. Brasília has trees. But they have yet to be convincing. They look plastic.

I am now going to write something of the utmost

importance: Brasília is the failure of the most spectacular success in the world. Brasília is a splattered star. It takes my breath away. It is beautiful and it is naked. The lack of shame one has in solitude. At the same time I was embarrassed to undress for a shower. As if a gigantic green eye were staring at me, implacable. Moreover Brasília is implacable. I felt as if someone were pointing at me: as if they could arrest me or take away my papers, my identity, my veracity, my last private breath. Oh what if the Radio Patrol catches me and beats me up! then I'll say the worst word in the Portuguese language: *sovaco*, armpit. And they'll drop dead. But for you, my love, I am more delicate and softly say: *axilas*, underarms . . .

Brasília smells like toothpaste. And whoever's not married, loves without passion. They simply have sex. But I want to return, I want to try to decipher its enigma. I want especially to talk with university students. I want them to invite me to participate in this aridness, luminous and full of stars. Does anyone ever die in Brasília? No. Never. No one ever dies because there you cannot close your eyes. There they have hibernation: the air leaves a person in a stupor for years, who later comes back to life. The climate is challenging and whips people a bit. But Brasília needs magic, it needs voodoo. I don't want Brasília to put a curse on me: because it would work. I pray. I pray a lot. Oh what a good God. Everything there is out in the open and whoever wants it has to deal with it. Though the rats adore the city. I wonder what they eat?

ah, I know: they eat human flesh. I escaped as best I could. And seemed to be remotely controlled.

I gave countless interviews. They changed what I said. I no longer give interviews. And if the whole business really is based on invading my privacy, then they should pay for it. They say that's how it's done in the United States. And another thing: there's one price just for me, but if my precious dog gets included, I charge extra. If they distort me, I charge a fine. Sorry, I have no wish to humiliate anyone but I have no wish to be humiliated. While there I said I might go to Colombia and they wrote that I was going to Bolivia. They switched the country for no reason. But there's no danger: all I concede about my own life is that I have two sons. I am not important, I am an average person who wants a little anonymity. I hate giving interviews. Come on, I am a woman who's simple and a tiny bit sophisticated. A mix of peasant and a star in the sky.

I adore Brasília. Is that contradictory? But what isn't contradictory? People only go down the deserted streets by car. When I had a car and drove, I was always getting lost. I never knew where I was coming from and where I was going. I am disoriented in life, in art, in time and in space. Unbelievable, for God's sake.

There people have dinner and lunch together – it is to have people to populate them. This is good and very pleasant. It is the slow humanization of a city that for some hidden reason is arduous. I really enjoyed it, they pampered me so much in Brasília. But there were some people who wanted me gone in a flash. I was tripping up their routine. For those people I was an inconvenient novelty. Living is dramatic. But there is no escaping it: we are born.

What will a person born in Brasília be like when he grows up and becomes a man? Because the city is inhabited by nostalgic outsiders. Exiles. Those born there will be the future. A future sparkling like steel. If I am still alive, I shall applaud the strange and highly novel product that will emerge. Will smoking be banned? Will everything be banned, my God? Brasília seems like an inauguration. Every day it is inaugurated. Festivities, my dears, festivities. Let them raise the flags.

Who wants me in Brasília? So whoever wants me can call me. Not just yet, because I am still stunned. But in a while. At your service. Brasília is at your service. I want to speak with the hotel maid who said to me when she found out who I was: I wanted to write so badly! I said: go on, woman, and write. She answered: but I've already suffered too much. I said severely: so go ahead and write about what you've suffered.

Because there needs to be someone crying in Brasília. The eyes of its inhabitants are much too dry. In that case – in that case I am volunteering to cry. My maid and I, we, girlfriends. She told me: when I saw you, ma'am, I got goosebumps on my arm. She told me she was a psychic.

Yes. I've got goosebumps. And I am shivering. God help me. I am mute like a moon.

Brasília is full-time. I have a panicked fear of it. It is the ideal place for taking a sauna. Sauna? Yes. Because there you don't know what to do with yourself. I look down, I look up, I look around – and the reply is a howl: nooooooooo! Brasília stupefies us so much it's scary. Why do I feel so guilty there? what did I do wrong? and why haven't they erected right in the city center a great white Egg? It is because there is no center. But it needs the Egg.

What kind of clothes do people wear in Brasília? Metallic?

Brasília is my martyrdom. And it has no nouns. It's all adjectives. And how it hurts. Ah, my dear little God, grant me just one little noun, for God's sake! Ah, you don't want to? then pretend I didn't say anything. I know how to lose.

Oh stewardess, try to give me a less numbered smile. Is that the sandwich we're supposed to eat? all dehydrated? But I'll do like Sérgio Porto: I heard that on a plane a stewardess once asked him: can I offer you some coffee, sir? And he answered: I'll take everything I have a right to.

In Brasília it is never night. It is always implacably day. Punishment? But what did I do wrong, my God? I don't want to hear it, He says, punishment is punishment.

In Brasília there is practically nowhere to drop dead. But there is one thing: Brasília is pure protein. Didn't I say that Brasília is a tennis court? Because Brasília is blood on a tennis court. And as for me? where am I? me? poor me, with my scarlet-stained handkerchief. Do I kill myself? No. I live in brute reply. I am right there for whoever wants me.

But Brasília is the opposite sound. And no one denies that Brasília is: goooooooooal! Though it slightly warps the samba. Who is that? who is that singing hallelujah and whom I hear with joy? Who is it that traverses, like the sharpest of swords, the future and always future city of Brasília? I repeat: pure protein, you are. You have fertilized me. Or am I the one singing? Listening to myself I am moved. There's Brasília in the air. In the air unfortunately lacking the indispensable support of corners for people to live. Have I already mentioned that nobody lives in Brasília? they reside. Brasília is bone dried out from pure astonishment under the merciless sun on the beach. Ah white horse but what a rustic mane. Oh, I can't wait any longer. A little airplane, please. And the ashen moonlight that enters the room and watches me, I, pale, white, cunning.

I don't have a corner. My transistor radio isn't picking up any music. What's wrong? Not that way either. Do I repeat myself? And does it hurt?

For the love of Cod (I was so startled I even mixed up the word God), for the love of God, please forgive me those of you who reside in Brasília for saying what I am forced to say, I, a lowly slave to the truth. I do not mean to offend anyone. It is just that the light is too white. I have sensitive eyes, I am invaded by the stark brightness and all that red land.

Brasília is a future that happened in the past.

Eternal as a stone. The light of Brasília – am I repeating myself? – the light of Brasília wounds my feminine modesty. That is all, people, that is all.

Aside from that, long live Brasília! I will help hoist the flag. And I will forgive the slap I got in my poor face. Oh, poor little me. So motherless. It is our duty to have a mother. It is a thing of nature. I am in favor of Brasília.

In the year 2000 there will be a celebration there. If I am still alive, I want to join in the revelry. Brasília is an exaggerated general revelry. A little hysterical, it's true, but that's fine. Bursts of laughter in the dark hallway. I laugh, you laugh, he laughs. Three.

In Brasília there are no lampposts for dogs to pee on. It badly needs a peepee-dog. But Brasília is a gem, dear sir. There everything works as it should. Brasília envelops me in gold. I'm off to the hairdresser. I'm talking about Rio. Hello, Rio! Hello! Hello! I really am frightened. God help me.

But there comes a time when I'll tell you, my friend, there comes a time when Brasília is a hair in your soup. I am very busy, Brasília, to hell with you and leave me alone. Brasília is located nowhere. Its atmosphere is indignation and you know why. Brasília: before being born it was already born, the premature, the unborn, the fetus, in a word me. Oh the nerve.

Not just anyone can enter Brasília, no. You need nobility, lots of shamelessness and lots of nobility. Brasília is not. It is merely the picture of itself. I love you, oh extragantic one! oh word I invented and do not know the meaning of. Oh furuncle! crystallized pus but whose? Warning: there's sperm in the air.

I, the scribe. I, fated to be the unfortunate definer. Brasília is the opposite of Bahia. Bahia is buttocks. Ah how I long for the soaked Place Vendôme. Ah, how I long for the Praça Maciel Pinheiro in Recife. So much poverty of soul. And you demand it of me. I, who can do nothing. Ah how I long for my dog. Such a dear friend. But a newspaper took his picture and he was standing at the end of the street. He and I. We, little brother and sister of St Francis of Assisi. Let us be silent: it is better for us.

I'm going to get you, Brasília! And you'll suffer terrible torture at my hands! You annoy me, o ice-cold Brasília, pearl among swine. Oh apocalyptic one.

And suddenly the big disgrace. All that racket. Why? Nobody knows. Oh God, how did I not see it right away? Because isn't Brasília 'Women's Health'? Brasília can't figure out what it wants: it's a tease. Brasília is a chipped tooth right in front. And it is the summit too. There is one main reason. What is it? secrets, lots of secrets, murmurs, whispers and whisps. Rumors that never end.

Healthy, healthy. Here I am a physical education teacher. I go tumbling. That's right: I raise hell. Brasília is a heavenly hell. It is a typewriter: click-click-click. I want to sleep! leave me alone!!! I am ti-i-red. Of being in-com-pre-hen-si-ble. But I do not want to be understood because I will lose my sacred intimacy. It is very serious, what I am saying, very serious indeed: Brasília is the ghost of an old blind man with a cane going click-click-click. And with no dog, poor guy. And me? how can I help? Brasília helps itself. It is a high-high-high-pitched violin. It needs a cello. But what a racket. This was surely uncalled for. I guarantee it. Though Brasília has no guarantor.

I want to return to Brasília to Room 700. So I can dot the 'i.' But Brasília does not flow. It goes in the opposite direction. Like this: wolf (flow).

It is mad yet functional. How I hate the word 'yet.' I only use it because it's needed.

When night falls Brasília becomes Zebedee. Brasília is a round-the-clock pharmacy.

The girl frisked me all over at the airport. I asked: do I look like a subversive? She said laughing: actually you do. I have never been so thoroughly felt up, Holy Mary, it's practically a sin. Her hands patted me down so much I don't know how I could stand it.

Brasília is slim. And utterly elegant. It wears a wig and false eyelashes. It is a scroll inside a Pyramid. It does not age. It is Coca-Cola, my God, and will outlive me. Too bad. For Coca-Cola, of course. Help! Help! *help me!* Do you know how Brasília answers my cry for help? It is formal: may I offer you some coffee? And what about me?

don't I get any help? Treat me well, got it? like that . . .
like that . . . nice and slow. That's it. That's it. What a
relief. Happiness, my dear, is relief. Brasília is a kick in
the rear. It is a place where the Portuguese get rich. And
what about me, who plays the lottery and doesn't win?

Oh what a pretty nose Brasília has. So delicate.

Did you know that Brasília is etc.? Well now you know.
Brasília is XPTR . . . as many consonants as you like but
not a single vowel to give you a break. And Brasília, well
dear sir, sorry, but Brasília left off right there.

Look, Brasília, I'm not just anyone, not at all. Show
more respect, do me the favor. I am a space traveler. I
demand lots of respect. Lots of Shakespeare. Ah but I
don't want to die! Oh, what a sigh. But Brasília is waiting.
And I can't stand waiting. Blue phantom. Ah, how annoying. It's like trying to remember and not being able to. I
want to forget Brasília but it won't let me. What a dried-
up wound. Gold. Brasília is gold. A gem. Sparkling. There
are things about Brasília that I know but can't say, they
won't let me. Guess.

And may God help me.

Go ahead, woman, go and fulfill your destiny, woman.
Being the woman I am is a duty. Right this instant-now
I am hoisting the flags – but what a fierce southern
wind! – and here I am saying hurrah!

Oh I am so tired.

In Brasília it is always Sunday. But now I am going to
speak very softly. Like this: my love. My great love. Have

I said it? You're the one who answers. I am going to end with the most beautiful word in the world. Nice and slow like this: my love how I have longed for you. L-o-v-e. I kiss you. Like a flower. Mouth to mouth. How bold. And now – now peace. Peace and life. I-am a-live. Maybe I don't deserve so much. I am afraid. But I don't want to end with fear. Ecstasy. *Yes, my love*. I surrender. Yes. *Pour toujours*. Everything – but everything is absolutely natural. *Yes*. I. But above all you are the guilty one, Brasília. However, I pardon you. It's not your fault you're so lovely and pitiful and poignant and mad. Yes, a wind of Justice is blowing. So I say to the Great Natural Law: yes. Hey cracked mirror: who is prettier than me? No one, the magic mirror replies. Yes, I am well aware, it's us two. Yes! yes! yes! I said yes.

I call humbly for help. They're robbing me. Am I the whole world? General astonishment. This isn't a high wind, sir, it's a tornado. I am in Rio. I finally got off the flying saucer. And a friend comes up saying – hello there Carmen Miranda! – telling me there's a song called 'Tar Baby Doll' that goes more or less like this: here I come all pinched with my aching corns, almost choking in my tight collar, to see my baby.

I have landed. My voice is weak but I will say what Brasília wants me to: bravo! bravíssimo! And that is enough. Now I am going to live in Rio with my dog. Please do me the favor of remaining silent. Like this: si-lence. I am so sad.

Brasília is a wildly twinkling blue eye that burns in my heart.

Brasília is Malta. Where is Malta? It's in the day of the super-never. Hello! hello! Malta! Today it's Sunday in New York. In Brasília, the gleaming one, it's already Tuesday. Brasília just skips Monday. Monday is the day you go to the dentist, what can you do, boring things have to get done too, woe is me. In Brasília I bet they're still dancing, unbelievable. It's six-twenty in the evening, almost night. At 6:20 nothing happens. Hello! Hello! Brasília! I want an answer, I'm in a hurry, I have just come to terms with my death. I am sad. The stride is too big for my legs though they are long. Help me die in peace. As I may have said, I want a beloved hand to hold mine when it is time for me to go. I go under protest. I. The phantasmagoric one. My name does not exist. What exists is a picture faked from another picture of me. But the real one died already. I died on the ninth of June. Sunday. After lunch in the precious company of those I love. I had roast chicken. I am happy. But lack true death. I am in a hurry to see God. Pray for me. I died elegantly.

I have a virgin soul and therefore need protection. Who will help me? The paroxysm of Chopin. Only you can help me. Deep down I am alone. There are truths I haven't even told God. And not even myself. I am a secret under the lock of seven keys. Please spare me. I am so alone. I and my rituals. The phone doesn't ring. It hurts. But God is the one who spares me. Amen.

Did you know that I can speak the language of dogs and also of plants? Amen. But my word is not the last. There exists one I cannot utter. And my tale is gallant. I am an anonymous letter. I do not sign the things I write. Let other people sign. I do not have the credentials. Me? But me of all people? Never! I need a father. Who will volunteer? No, I do not need a father, I need my equal. I am waiting for death. Oh such wind, dear sir. Wind is a thing you cannot see. I ask Our Lord God Jehovah about his wrath in the form of wind. Only He can explain. Or can he? If He cannot, I am lost. Oh how I love you and I love so much that I die you.

Remember how I mentioned the tennis court with blood? Well the blood was mine, the scarlet, the clotting was mine.

Brasília is a horse race. No I am not a horse. Brasília can go to hell and run by itself without me.

Brasília is hyperbolic. I am suspended until the final order. I survive by being as stubborn as I am. I have landed indeed. *There is no place like home.* How good it is to be back. Leaving is good but coming back is more better. That's right: more better.

What is supplementary in Brasília? No I don't know, dear sir. All I know is that all is nothing and nothing is all. My dog is sleeping. I am my dog. I call myself Ulisses. We are both tired. So, so tired. Woe is me, woe is us. Silence. You should sleep too. Ah astonished city. It astonishes itself. I am feeling stale. What I'll do is complain like Chopin complained about the invasion of Poland. After all I have my rights. I am I, that's what other people say. And if they say so, why not believe it? Farewell. I'm fed up. I'm going to complain. I'm going to complain to God. And if He can, let him heed me. I am one of the needy. I left Brasília with a cane. Today is Sunday. Even God rested. God is a funny thing: He can do it all for Himself and needs Himself.

I came home, it is true, but wouldn't you know my cook writes literature? I asked her where the Coca-Cola in the fridge was. She answered, lovely black girl that she is: she was just so tired, so I made her go rest, poor thing. Once, ages ago I recounted to Paulo Mendes Campos a comment my maid at the time had made. And he wrote something like this: everyone gets the maid they deserve: My maid has a beautiful voice and sings to me when I ask her to: 'Nobody Loves Me.' She draws, she writes. I am so humbled. For I don't deserve this much.

I am nothing. I am a frustrated Sunday. Or am I being ungrateful? Much has been given me, much has been taken away. Who wins? Not me that's for sure. Someone hyperbolic does.

Brasília, be a little bit animal too. It's so nice. So very nice. Not having peepee-dogs is an affront to my dog who will never go to Brasília for obvious reasons. It's a quarter to six. No particular time. Even Kissinger is asleep. Or is he on a plane? There's no way to guess. Happy birthday, Kissinger. Happy birthday, Brasília. Brasília is a mass suicide. Brasília, are you scratching yourself? not me, I don't go in for that kind of thing because whoever starts won't stop from. You know the rest.

The rest is paroxysm.

No one knows it, but my dog not only smokes but also drinks coffee and eats flowers. And drinks beer. He also takes antidepressants. He resembles a little mulatto. What he needs is a girlfriend. He's middle class. I didn't let the newspaper in on everything. But now it's time for the truth. You too should have the courage to read. The only thing this dog doesn't do is write. He eats pens and shreds paper. Better than I do. He is my animal son. He was born of the instantaneous contact between the Moon and a mare. Mare of the Sun. He is a thing Brasília is not. He is: an animal. I am an animal. I really want to repeat myself, just to annoy people.

My God, I've gone back in time. It's exactly twenty to six. And I answer the typewriter: *yes*. The monstrous typewriter. It's a telescope. Such wind. Is it a tornado? It is.

Oh what a place to look pretty. Today is Monday, the tenth. As you can see, I didn't die. I am going to the dentist. A dangerous week, this one. I am telling the truth. Not the whole truth, as I said. And if God knows it, that's His business. Let him deal with it. I don't know how but I am going to deal as best I can. Like a cripple. Living for free is what you cannot do. Pay to live? I am living on borrowed time. Just like that mutt Ulisses. As for me, I think that.

How embarrassing. It is my case of public embarrassment. I have three bison in my life. One plus one plus one plus one plus one. The fourth kills me in Malta. In fact the seventh is the shiniest. Bison, if you didn't know, are cave-dwelling animals. I perform my stories. Human warmth. Fearless city, that one. God is the hour. I am going to last a while yet. No one is immortal. Just see if you can find someone who doesn't die.

I died. I died murdered by Brasília. I died to pursue research. Pray for me because I died on my back.

Look, Brasília, I left. And God help me. It's because I am slightly before. That's all. I swear to God. And I am slightly after too. What can you do. Brasília is broken glass on the street. Shards. Brasília is a dentist's metal tool. And very motorcycle too. Which doesn't stop it from being mullet roe, fried up with plenty of salt. I just happen to be so eager for life, I want so much from it and I take advantage of it so much and everything is so much – that I become immoral. That's right: I am immoral. How nice to be unsuitable for those eighteen and under.

Brasília exercises every day at 5 a.m. The Bahians there are the only ones who don't go in for that kind of thing. They write poetry.

Brasília is the mystery categorized in steel filing cabinets. Everything there is categorized. And me? who am I? how have they categorized me? Have they given me a number? I feel numbered, and constricted all over. I barely fit inside myself. I am just a little me, very unimportant. But with a certain class.

Being happy is such a great responsibility. Brasília is happy. It has the nerve. What will become of Brasília in the year, let us say, 3000? How big a pile of bones. No one remembers the future because it's not possible. The authorities won't allow it. And me, who am I? Out of pure fear I obey the most insignificant soldier who stands before me and says: you're under arrest. Oh I'm going to cry. I am barely. *On the verge of.*

It's becoming clear that I don't know how to describe Brasília. It is Jupiter. It is a word well chosen. It is too grammatical for my taste. And the worst thing is it demands grammar *but I don't know, sir, I don't know the rules.*

Brasília is an airport. The loudspeakers coldly and courteously announce the departing flights.

What else? the thing is, no one knows what to do in Brasília. The only ones who do anything are the people who work like crazy, who make babies like crazy and get together like crazy to dine on the finest delicacies.

I stayed at the Hotel Nacional. Room 800. And drank Coca-Cola in my room. I am constantly – fool that I am – giving away free advertising.

At seven in the evening I will speak just superficially about avant-garde Brazilian literature, since I am not a critic. God spare me from critiquing. I have a morbid fear of facing people who are listening to me. Electrified. Speaking of which Brasília is electrified and a computer.

I am definitely going to read too fast so I can get through it quickly. I will be introduced to the audience by José Guilherme Merquior. Merquior is much too wholesome. I feel honored and at the same time so humble. After all, who am I to face a demanding public? I'll do what I can. Once I gave a talk at the Catholic University and Affonso Romano de Sant'Anna, I don't know what got into that fabulous critic, asked me a question: does two plus two equal five? For a second I was speechless. But then a darkly humorous anecdote sprang to mind: It goes like this: the psychotic says that two plus two equals five. The neurotic says: two plus two equals four but I just can't take it. Then there was laughter and everyone relaxed.

Tomorrow I return to Rio, turbulent city of my loves. I like to fly: I love speed. With Vicente I got him to zip around Brasília very fast by car. I sat beside him and we talked a lot. See you later: I'm going to read while waiting to be picked up for the conference. In Brasília you feel like looking pretty. I felt like getting all done up. Brasília is risky and I love risk. It's an adventure: it brings me face to face with the unknown. I'm going to speak words. Words have nothing to do with sensations. Words are hard stones and sensations are ever so delicate, fleeting, extreme. Brasília became humanized. Only I can't stand those rounded streets, that vital lack of corners. There, even the sky is rounded. The clouds are agnus dei. Brasília's air is so *dry* that the skin on your face gets dry, your hands rough.

The dentist's machine called 'Atlas 200' says this to me: tchi! tchi! tchi! Today is the 14th. Fourteen leaves me suspended. Brasília is fifteen point one. Rio is one, but a tiny one. Doesn't Atlas 200 ever die? No, it doesn't. It is like me when I am hibernating in Brasília.

Brasília is an orange construction crane fishing out something very delicate: a small white egg. Is that white egg me or a little child born today?

I feel like people are working voodoo on me: who wants to steal my poor identity? All I'll do is this: I'll ask for help and have some coffee. Then I'll smoke. Oh how I smoked and smoked in Brasília! Brasília is a Hollywood-brand filtered cigarette. Brasília is like this: right now I am listening to the sound of the key in the front door lock. A mystery? A mystery, yes sir. I go open it and guess who it was? it was nobody. Brasília is somebody, red carpet, tails and a top hat.

Brasília is a pair of stainless steel scissors. I save what I can to make ends meet. And I have already drawn up my will. I say a bunch of things in it.

Brasília is the sound of ice cubes in a glass of whiskey, at six in the evening, the hour of nobody.

Do you want me to tell Brasília: here's to you? I say here's to you with the glass in my hand. In Rio, in my pantry, I killed a mosquito that was quivering in midair. Why this right to kill? It was merely a flying atom. Never will I forget that mosquito whose destiny I plotted, I, the one without a destiny.

I am tired, listening at dawn to the Ministry of Education that also comes from Brasília. Right now I am listening to the Blue Danube in whose waters I recline, serious and alert.

Brasília is science fiction. Brasília is Ceará turned inside out: both bruising and conquering.

And it is a chorus of children on an incredibly blue, super cold morning, the kids opening their little round mouths and intoning an utterly innocent Te Deum, accompanied by organ music. I wish this would happen in the stained glass church at 7 in the evening. Or 7 in the morning. I prefer morning, since twilight in Brasília is more beautiful than the involuntary sunset in Porto Alegre. Brasília is a first place on the university entrance exams. I'm happy with just a little ol' second place.

I see that I wrote seven as a numeral: 7. Well Brasília is 7. It's 3. It's four. It's eight, nine – I'm skipping the others, and at 13 I meet God.

The problem is that blank paper demands I write. I'll go ahead and write. Alone in the world, high on a hill. I would like to conduct an orchestra, but they say women can't because they don't have the physical stamina. Ah, Schubert, sweeten up Brasília a little. I'm so good to Brasília.

Right this instant-now it's ten to seven. *Me muero.* Make yourself at home, dear sir, and the service I offer is deluxe. Whoever wants to can live it up. Brasília is a five-hundred-cruzeiro bill that nobody wants to break. And

161

the number 1 penny? that one I insist on keeping for myself. It's so rare. It brings good luck. And it brings privileges. Five hundred cruzeiros go down my throat.

Brasília is different. Brasília is inviting. And if invited, I'll attend. Brasília uses a diamond-studded cigarette holder.

But it is common for people to say: I want money and I want to die suddenly. Even me. But St Francis took off all his clothes and went naked. He and my dog Ulisses ask for nothing. Brasília is a pact I made with God.

All I ask is one favor, Brasília, of you: don't take up speaking Esperanto. Don't you see that words get distorted in Esperanto as in a badly translated translation? *Yes, my Lord. I said yes, sir. I almost said: my love*, instead of *my Lord. But my love is my Lord. There is no answer? O.K., I can stand It.* But how it hurts. It hurts so much to be offended by not getting a reply. I can take it. But don't anyone step on my feet because that hurts. And I am on familiar terms, I go by my first name, don't stand on ceremony. It'll go like this: I address you as honorable sir and you use my first name. You are so gallant, Brasília.

Does Brasília have a botanical garden? and does it have a zoo? It needs them, because people cannot live on man alone. Having animals around is essential.

Where is your tragic opera, Brasília? I won't accept operettas, they are too nostalgic, lead soldiers are what I used to play with, despite being a girl. The blues gently shatters my heart that even so is as hot as the blues itself.

Brasília is Physical Law. Relax, ma'am, take off your girdle, don't get flustered, have a little sip of sugar water – and then see what it's like to be Natural Law a little. You'll love it, ma'am.

Does there happen to exist a course of study called Course on the Existence of Time? Well it should.

Well didn't they pour bleach on the ground in Brasília. Well they did: to disinfect. But I am, thank God, thoroughly infected. But I had my lungs x-rayed and said to the doctor: my lungs must be black from smoke. He answered: well actually they aren't, they're nice and clear.

And so it goes on. I am suddenly silent and have nothing to say. Respect my silence. I don't paint, no ma'am, I write and do I ever.

In Brasília I didn't dream. Could it be my fault or does no one dream in Brasília? And that hotel maid? what became of her? I too have suffered, you hear, maid-woman? Suffering is the privilege of those who feel. But now I am sheer joy. It's almost six in the morning. I got up at four. I am wide awake. Brasília is wide awake. Pay attention to what I am saying: Brasília will never end. I die and Brasília remains. With new people, of course. Brasília is hot off the press.

Brasília is the Wedding March. The groom is a north-easterner who eats up the whole cake because he's gone hungry for several generations. The bride is a widowed old lady, rich and cranky. From this unusual wedding that I witnessed, forced by circumstances, I left defeated by

163

the violence of the Wedding March that sounded like a Military March and commanded me to get married too and I don't want to. I left covered in Band-Aids, my ankle twisted, my neck aching and a big wound aching in my heart.

Everything I have said is true. Or it is symbolic. But what difficult syntax Brasília has! The fortuneteller said I would go to Brasília. She knows everything, Dona Nadir, from Méier. Brasília is an eyelid fluttering like the yellow butterfly I saw a few days ago on the corner near my house. Yellow butterflies are a good omen. Geckos say neither yes nor no. But S. has a fear of geckos who are shedding their skin. What I am more afraid of are rats. At the Hotel Nacional they guaranteed they didn't have rats. So, in that case, I stayed. With a guarantee, I often stay.

Working is fate. Look, *Jornal de Brasília*, you better include astrology in your paper. After all, we need to know where we stand. I am completely magical and my aura is bright blue just like the sweet stained glass in the church I mentioned. Everything I touch, is born.

It is daybreak here in Rio. A lovely and cold dry morning. How nice that all nights have radiant mornings. Brasília's horoscope is dazzling. And whoever wants to, let them bear it.

It's a quarter to six. I write while listening to music. Anything will do, I'm not difficult. What I was hoping to hear right now was a really astringent fado sung by Amália Rodrigues in Lisbon. Ah how I long for Capri. I suffered so much in Capri. But I forgave it. It's all right: Capri, like Brasília, is beautiful. I do feel sorry for Brasília because it doesn't have the sea. But the salt wind is in the air. I detest swimming in a pool. Swimming in the sea breeds courage. A few days ago I went to the beach and entered the sea feeling moved. I drank seven gulps of saltwater from the sea. The water was chilly, gentle, with little waves that were also agnus dei. I am letting you know that I am going to buy an old-fashioned felt hat, with a small crown and upturned brim. And also a green crocheted shawl. Brasília isn't crochet, it is a knit made by special machines that don't make errors. But, as I said, I am pure error. And I have a left-handed soul. I get all tangled in emerald-green crochet, I get all tangled. To protect myself. Green is the color of hope. And Tuesday could be a disaster. On my last Tuesday I cried because I had been wronged. But in general Tuesdays are good. As for Thursday, it is sweet and a little bit sad. Laugh all you want, clown, as your house catches fire. *Mais tout va très bien, madame la Marquise.* Except.

Could there be fauns in Brasília? That settles it: what I'll do is buy a green hat to match my shawl. Or should I not buy one at all? I am so indecisive. Brasília is decision. Brasília is a man. And I, such a woman. I go bumbling along. I stumble into something here, I stumble into something there. And arrive at last.

The song I am listening to now is completely pure and free of guilt. Debussy. With cool little waves in the sea.

Does Brasília have gnomes?

My house in Rio is full of them. All fantastic. Try just one gnome and you'll be hooked. Elves also do the trick. Dwarves? I feel sorry for them.

I've settled it: I don't need a hat at all. Or do I? My God, what shall become of me? Brasília, save me for I am in need of it.

One day I was a child just like Brasília. And I so badly wanted a carrier pigeon. To send letters to Brasília. Does anyone get them? yes or no?

I am innocent and ignorant. And when I am in writing mode, I don't read. That would be too much for me, I don't have the strength.

I was on the plane with an older Portuguese gentleman, a businessman of some sort, but very genteel: he carried my heavy suitcase. On the way back from Brasília I sat next to an older gentleman who was such a good conversationalist, we had such a good conversation, that I said: it's incredible how fast the time went and now we're here. He said: the time went fast for me too. I'll see that man some day. He's going to teach me. He knows a lot of things.

I am so lost. But that is exactly how we live: lost in time and space.

I am scared to death of appearing before a Judge. Your Most Esteemed Honor, may I have permission to smoke? Yes, indeed ma'am, I myself smoke a pipe. Thank you, Your Eminence. I treat the Judge well, a Judge is Brasília. But I won't sue Brasília. It hasn't wronged me.

We are in the middle of the world cup. There is an African country that is poor and ignorant and lost to Yugoslavia 9 to zero. But their ignorance is different: I heard that in that country the black boys either win or they die. Such helplessness.

I know how to die. I have been dying since I was little. And it hurts but we pretend it doesn't. I miss God so badly.

And now I am going to die a little bit. I need to so much.

Yes. I accept, *my Lord*. Under protest.

But Brasília is splendor.

I am utterly afraid.

Beauty and the Beast or
The Enormous Wound

IT BEGINS:

Well, so she left the beauty salon by the elevator in the Copacabana Palace Hotel. Her driver wasn't there. She looked at her watch: it was four in the afternoon. And suddenly she remembered: she'd told 'her' José to pick her up at five, not factoring in that she wouldn't get a manicure or pedicure, just a massage. What should she do? Take a taxi? But she had a five-hundred-cruzeiro bill on her and the cab driver wouldn't have change. She'd brought cash because her husband had told her you should never go out without cash. It crossed her mind to go back to the beauty salon and ask for change. But – but it was a May afternoon and the cool air was a flower blooming with its perfume. And so she thought it wonderful and unusual to be standing on the street – out in the wind that was ruffling her hair. She couldn't remember the last time she'd been alone with herself. Maybe never. It was always her – with others, and in these others she was reflected and the others were reflected in her. Nothing was – was pure, she thought without understanding what she meant. When she saw herself in the mirror – her skin, tawny from sunbathing, made the gold flowers in her black hair stand out against her face – she held back from exclaiming 'ah!' – for she was fifty million units of beautiful people. Never had there been – in all the world's history – anyone like her. And then, in three trillion trillion years – there wouldn't be a single girl exactly like her.

'I am a burning flame! And I shine and shine all that darkness!'

This moment was unique – and she would have in the course of her life thousands of unique moments. Her forehead even broke out in a cold sweat, because so much had been given her and eagerly taken by her.

'Beauty can lead to the kind of madness that is passion.' She thought: 'I am married, I have three children, I am safe.'

She had a name to uphold: it was Carla de Sousa e Santos. The 'de' and the 'e' were important: they denoted class and a four-hundred-year-old Rio family. She lived among the herds of women and men who, yes, who simply 'could.' Could what? Look, they just could. And to top it off, they were slick because their 'could' was just so greasy in the machines that ran without the sound of rusty metal. She, who was a powerful woman. A generator of electric energy. She, who made use of the vineyards on her country estate to relax. She possessed traditions in decay but still standing. And since there was no new criterion to sustain all those vague and grandiose hopes, the weighty tradition still held. Tradition of what? Of nothing, if you had to pry. The only argument in its favor was the fact that the inhabitants were backed by a long lineage, which, though plebeian, was enough to grant them a certain pose of dignity.

She thought, all tangled: She who, being a woman, which seemed to her a funny thing to be or not to be, knew that, if she were a man, she'd naturally be a banker, a normal thing that happens among 'her' people, that is, those of her social class, which her husband, on the other hand, had attained after a lot of hard work and which classified him as a 'self-made man' whereas she was not a 'self-made woman.' At the end of the long train of thought, it seemed to her that – that she hadn't been thinking about anything.

A man missing a leg, dragging himself along on a crutch, stopped before her and said:

'Miss, won't you give me some money so I can eat?'

'Help!!!' she screamed in her head upon seeing the enormous wound in the man's leg. 'Help me, God,' she said very softly.

She was exposed to that man. She was completely exposed. Had she told 'her' José to come to the exit on the Avenida Atlântica, the hotel where the hairdresser's was wouldn't have allowed 'those people' to come near. But on the Avenida Copacabana anything was possible: people of every sort. At least a different sort from hers. 'Hers'? What sort of she was she for it to be 'hers'?

She – the others. But, but death doesn't separate us, she thought suddenly and her face took on the aspect of a mask of beauty and not human beauty: her face hardened for a moment.

The beggar's thoughts: 'this lady with all that makeup and little gold stars on her forehead, either won't give me anything or just a little.' It struck him then, a bit wearily: 'or next to nothing.'

She was alarmed: since she practically never walked down the street – she was chauffeured from door to door – she started thinking: is he going to kill me? She was distraught and asked:

'How much do people usually give?'

'However much they can and want to,' answered the shocked beggar.

She, who never paid at the beauty salon, the manager there sent her monthly bill to her husband's secretary. 'Husband.' She thought: her husband, what would he do with the beggar? She knew what: nothing. They don't do anything. And she – she was 'them' too. All that she could give? She could give her husband's bank, she might give him their apartment, her country house, her jewelry . . .

But something that was a greed in everyone, asked:

'Is five hundred cruzeiros enough? That's all I have.'

The beggar stared at her in shock.

'Are you making fun of me, miss?'

'Me?? No I'm not, I really do have the five hundred in my purse . . .'

She opened it, pulled out the bill and humbly handed it to the man, nearly begging his pardon.

The man bewildered.

And then laughing, showing his nearly toothless gums: 'Look,' he said, 'either you're very kind, ma'am, or you're not right in the head . . . But, I'll take it, don't go saying later that I robbed you, no one's gonna believe me. It would've been better if you gave me some change.'

'I don't have any change, all I have is that five hundred.'

The man seemed to get scared, he said something nearly incomprehensible, garbled from his having so few teeth.

Meanwhile his head was thinking: food, food, good food, money, money.

Her head was full of parties, parties, parties. Celebrating what? Celebrating someone else's wound? One thing united them: both had a vocation for money. The beggar spent every cent he had, whereas Carla's husband, the banker, accumulated money. His bread and butter was the Stock Market, and inflation, and profit. The beggar's bread and butter was his round gaping wound. And to top it off, he was probably afraid of healing, she guessed, because, if it got better, he'd have nothing to eat, that much Carla knew: 'if you don't have a good job by a certain age . . .' If he were younger, he could paint walls. Since he wasn't, he invested in that big wound with living and pestilent flesh. No, life wasn't pretty.

*

She leaned against the wall and decided to think carefully. It was different because she wasn't in the habit and she didn't know thought was vision and comprehension and that no one could order herself to do it just like that: think! Fine. But it so happened that deciding to posed an obstacle. So then she started looking inside herself and they actually started happening. Only, she had the most ridiculous thoughts. Like: does that beggar speak English? Has that beggar ever eaten caviar, while drinking champagne? They were ridiculous thoughts because she clearly knew the beggar didn't speak English, nor had he ever tasted caviar or champagne. But she couldn't help watching another absurd thought arise in her: had he ever skied in Switzerland?

She grew desperate then. She grew so desperate that a thought came to her made of just two words: 'Social Justice.'

Death to the rich! That would solve things, she thought cheerfully. But – who would give money to the poor?

Suddenly – suddenly everything stopped. The buses stopped, the cars stopped, the clocks stopped, the people on the street froze – only her heart was beating, and for what?

She saw that she didn't know how to deal with the world. She was an incompetent person, with her black hair and her long, red nails. She was: as if in a blurry color photograph. Every day she made a list of what she needed or wanted to do the next day – that was how she'd stayed connected to the empty hours. She simply had nothing to do. Everything was done for her. Even her two children – well, her husband was the one who had decided they'd have two . . .

'You've got to make an effort to be a winner in life,' her late grandfather had told her. Was she, by any chance, a 'winner'? If winning meant standing on the street in the middle of the bright afternoon, her face smeared with makeup and gold spangles . . . Was that winning? What patience she needed to have with herself. What patience she needed in order to save her own little life. Save it from what? Judgment? But who was judging? Her mouth felt completely dry and her throat on fire – just like whenever she had to take tests in school. And there was no water! Do you know what that's like – not having water?

She wanted to think about something else and forget the difficult present moment. Then she recalled lines from a posthumous book by Eça de Queirós that she'd studied in high school: 'Lake TIBERIAS shimmered transparently, covered in silence, bluer than the heavens, ringed entirely by flowering meadows, dense groves, rocks of porphyry, and pristine white lands among the palms, beneath the doves in flight.'

She knew it by heart because, as a teenager, she'd been very sensitive to words and because she'd desired for herself the same shimmering destiny as Lake TIBERIAS.

*

She felt an unexpectedly murderous urge: to kill all the beggars in the world! Just so she, after the massacre, could enjoy her extraordinary well-being in peace.

No. The world wasn't whispering.

The world was scre-am-ing!!! through that man's toothless mouth.

The banker's young wife thought she wasn't going to withstand the lack of softness being hurled in her impeccably made-up face.

And what about the party? How would she bring it up at the party, while dancing, how would she tell the partner who'd be in her arms . . . This: look, the beggar has a sex too, he said he had eleven children. He doesn't go to social gatherings, he doesn't appear in Ibrahim's society columns, or in Zózimo's, he's hungry for bread not cake, actually all he should eat is porridge since he doesn't have any teeth for chewing meat . . . 'Meat?' She vaguely recalled that the cook had said the price of filet mignon had gone up. Yes. How could she dance? Only if it were a mad and macabre beggars' dance.

No, she wasn't the kind of woman prone to hysteria and nerves and fainting or feeling ill. Like some of her little society 'colleagues.' She smiled a little thinking in terms of her little 'colleagues.' Colleagues in what? in dressing up? in hosting dinners for thirty, forty people?

She herself taking advantage of the garden in late summer had thrown a reception for how many guests? No, she didn't want to think about that, she recalled (why without the same pleasure?) the tables dispersed over the lawn, candlelight . . . 'candlelight'? she thought, but am I out of my mind? have I fallen for a scam? Some rich people's scam?

'Before I got married I was middle class, secretary to the banker I married and now – now candlelight. What I'm doing is playing at living,' she thought, 'this isn't life.'

'Beauty can be a great threat.' Extreme grace got mixed up with a bewilderment and a deep melancholy. 'Beauty frightens.' 'If I weren't so pretty I'd have had a different fate,' she thought arranging the gold flowers in her jet black hair.

She'd once seen a friend whose heart got all twisted up and hurt and mad with forceful passion. So she'd never wanted to experience it. She had always been frightened of things that were too beautiful or too horrible: because she didn't inherently know how to respond to them and whether she would respond if she were equally beautiful or equally horrible.

She was frightened as when she'd seen the Mona Lisa's smile, right there, up close at the Louvre. As she'd been frightened by the man with the wound or the man's wound.

She felt like screaming at the world: 'I'm not awful! I'm a product of I don't even know what, how can I know anything about this misery of the soul.'

To shift her feelings – since she couldn't bear them and now felt like, in despair, violently kicking the beggar's wound – to shift her feelings she thought: this is my second marriage, I mean, my previous husband was alive.

Now she understood why she'd married the first time and was auctioned off: who'll bid higher? who'll bid higher? Sold, then. Yes, she'd married the first time to the man who 'bid the highest,' she accepted him because he was rich and slightly above her social class. She had sold herself. And as for her second husband? Her second marriage was on the rocks, he had two mistresses . . . and she putting up with it all because a separation would have been scandalous: her name was mentioned too often in the society pages. And would she go back to her maiden name? Even getting used to her maiden name, that would take a long time. Anyway, she thought laughing at herself, anyway, she tolerated this second one because he gave her great prestige. Had she sold herself to the society pages? Yes. She was discovering that now. If there were a third marriage in store for her – for she was pretty and rich – if there were, whom would she marry? She started laughing a little hysterically because she had the thought: her third husband was the beggar.

Suddenly she asked the beggar:

'Sir, do you speak English?'

The man didn't have a clue what she'd asked. But, forced to answer since the woman had just bought him with all that money, he improvised:

'Yes I do. Well aren't I speaking with you right now, ma'am? Why? Are you deaf? Then I'll shout: YES.'

Alarmed by the man's ear-splitting shouts, she broke into a cold sweat. She was becoming fully aware that up till now she'd pretended there were no starving people, no people who don't speak any foreign languages and that there were no anonymous masses begging in order to survive. She'd known it, yes, but she'd turned her head and covered her eyes. Everyone, but everyone – knows and pretends they don't. And even if they didn't they'd feel a certain distress. How could they not? No, they wouldn't even feel that.

She was . . .

After all who was she?

No comment, especially since the question lasted a fraction of a second: question and answer hadn't been thoughts in her head, but in her body.

I am the Devil, she thought remembering what she'd learned in childhood. And the beggar is Jesus. But – what he wants isn't money, it's love, that man has lost his way from humanity just as I too have lost mine.

She wanted to force herself to understand the world and could only manage to remember snippets of remarks from her husband's friends: 'those power plants won't be enough.' What power plants, good Lord? the ones that belonged to Minister Galhardo? would he own power plants? 'Electric energy . . . hydroelectric'?

And the essential magic of living – where was it now? In what corner of the world? in the man sitting on the corner?

Is money what makes the world go round? she asked herself. But she wanted to pretend it wasn't. She felt so, so rich that she felt a certain pang.

The beggar's thoughts: 'Either that woman's crazy or she stole the money because there's no way she can be a millionaire,' millionaire was just a word to him and even if he wanted to see a millionaire in this woman he wouldn't have been able to because: who's ever seen a millionaire just standing around on the street, people? So he thought: what if she's one of those high-class hookers who charges their customers a lot and must be keeping some kind of religious vow?

Then.

Then.

Silence.

But suddenly that screaming thought:

'How did I never realize I'm a beggar too? I've never asked for spare change but I beg for the love of my husband who has two mistresses, I beg for God's sake for people to think I'm pretty, cheerful and acceptable, and my soul's clothing is in tatters . . .'

'There are things that equalize us,' she thought desperately seeking another point of equality. The answer suddenly came: they were equal because they'd been born and they both would die. They were, therefore, brother and sister.

She felt like saying: look, man, I'm a poor wretch too, the only difference is that I'm rich. I . . . she thought ferociously, I'm about to undermine money threatening my husband's credit in the market. I'm about to, any moment now, sit right on the curb. Being born was my worst disgrace. Now that I've paid for that accursed event, I feel I have a right to everything.

She was afraid. But suddenly she took the great leap of her life: courageously she sat on the ground.

'I bet she's a communist!' the beggar thought half believing it. 'And if she's a communist I'd have a right to her jewels, her apartments, her money and even her perfumes.'

Never again would she be the same person. Not that she'd never seen a beggar before. But – even this came at the wrong time, as if someone had jostled her and made her spill red wine all down a white lace dress. Suddenly she knew: that beggar was made of the same substance as she. Simple as that. The 'why' was what made the difference. On a physical level they were equal. As for her, she had an average education, and he didn't seem to know anything, not even who the President of Brazil was. She, however, had a keen capacity for understanding. Could it be that till now she'd possessed a buried intelligence? But what if she had just recently, coming into contact with a wound begging for money in order to eat – started thinking only of money? Money, which had always been obvious for her. And the wound, she'd never seen it so close up . . .

'Are you feeling bad, ma'am?'

'Not bad . . . but not good, I don't know . . .'

She thought: the body is a thing that, when ill, we carry. The beggar carries himself by himself.

'Today at the party? you'll feel better and everything will go back to normal,' said José.

Really at the party she'd refresh her attractiveness and everything would go back to normal.

She sat in the backseat of the air-conditioned car, casting before she left a final glance at that companion of an hour and a half. It seemed hard for her to say goodbye to him, he was now her alter ego 'I,' he was forever a part of her life. Farewell. She was dreamy, distracted, her lips parted as if a word were hanging there. For some reason she couldn't have explained – she was truly herself. And just like that, when the driver turned on the radio, she heard that codfish produced nine thousand eggs per year. She could deduce nothing from that statement, she who was in need of a destiny. She remembered how as a teenager she sought a destiny and chose to sing. As part of her upbringing, they easily found her a good teacher. But she sang badly, she herself knew it and her father, an opera lover, pretended not to notice that she sang badly. But there was a moment when she started to cry. Her perplexed teacher asked her what the matter was.

'It's just, it's just, I'm scared of, of, of, of singing well . . .'

But you sing very badly, the teacher had told her.

'I'm also scared, I'm also scared of singing much, much, much worse. Baaaaad way too bad!' she wailed and never had another singing lesson. That stuff about seeking art in order to understand had only happened to her once – afterward she had plunged into a forgetting that only now, at the age of thirty-five, through that wound, she needed either to sing very badly or very well – she was disoriented. How long since she had listened to so-called classical music because it might pull her out of the automatic sleep in which she lived. I – I'm playing at living. Next month she was going to New York and she realized the trip was like a new lie, like a daze. Having a wound in your leg – that's a reality. And everything in her life, since she was born, everything in her life had been soft like the leap of a cat.

(In the moving car)

Suddenly she thought: I didn't even think to ask his name.

Guy de Maupassant · *Moonlight* · 9780241619803

Carson McCullers · *The Ballad of the Sad Café* · 9780241590546

Yukio Mishima · *Death in Midsummer* · 9780241630853

Vladimir Nabokov · *Nabokov's Dozen* · 9780241630884

Anaïs Nin · *A Spy in the House of Love* · 9780241614686

George Orwell · *Shooting an Elephant* · 9780241630099

Dorothy Parker · *Big Blonde* · 9780241609934

Edgar Allan Poe · *The Masque of the Red Death* · 9780241573754

Alexander Pushkin · *The Queen of Spades* · 9780241573761

Rainer Maria Rilke · *Letters to a Young Poet* · 9780241620038

Françoise Sagan · *Bonjour Tristesse* · 9780241630891

Saki · *Reginald's Christmas Revel* · 9780241597026

Arthur Schnitzler · *Dream Story* · 9780241620229

Sam Selvon · *Calypso in London* · 9780241630877

Georges Simenon · *My Friend Maigret* · 9780241630792

John Steinbeck · *Of Mice and Men* · 9780241620236

Leo Tolstoy · *The Cossacks* · 9780241573778

Yuko Tsushima · *Territory of Light* · 9780241620243

Sylvia Townsend Warner · *Lolly Willowes* · 9780241573785

Edith Wharton · *Summer* · 9780241630815

Oscar Wilde · *The Star-Child* · 9780241597033

Virginia Woolf · *Street Haunting* · 9780241597040

Stefan Zweig · *Chess* · 9780241630822

For rights reasons, not all titles available in the USA and Canada.